# Severed Ties II

## Lenores's Revenge

**Gregory T. Glading**

# Acknowledgment

Severed Ties is a project that has spanned thirty years. After writing three drafts, I had abandoned hope of it seeing the light of day. The hard drive containing the final draft had crashed years ago. All soft copies of Severed Ties were long lost. All that remained was a paper manuscript stored in an old wooden barn. Even the hard copy manuscript disappeared. One day, a thorough house cleaning found the manuscript buried in my son's closet under a pile of long-discarded football gear. American Author's House, after publishing Darka's Quest, believed in my writing enough to take a chance on Severed Ties. Before submitting it for publication, I rewrote the entire novel a fourth time. Through the decades since writing the first word of Severed Ties to my approval of the final edited copy, many have advised me. Some of the advice was harsh and humbling, albeit beneficial and worthwhile. I am saddened that many who helped me develop my writing craft in general and Severed Ties in particular are no longer with us to see it as a book. Nevertheless, converting a quarter-century-old paper manuscript to a usable electronic format took technical skill well beyond my knowledge. A Lakeland, Florida firm called Computer Espresso worked wonders in converting the PDF scan into a Word document. I wish to acknowledge American Author's House in general for the task of turning the word conversion into a book-ready transcription. I want to acknowledge my technical manager, Lena Gray, in particular. She gave constant updates on the progress of the project. In addition, she would listen to my feedback and deftly relay it to her technical and editing staff to ensure that the job gets done properly.

# Contents

# Prologue

Lenore stared at the candlelight. Each flicker cast a new shadow on her face. She looked beyond the candlelight to a wall mirror. She grinned at her reflection. "They treated me like a peasant at college. I rose above them and became their queen. Football? Huh. Once that ended, so did my reign. I may be at the bottom now, but I'm rid of them both. Nothing will stop me now. I will take my rightful place and fulfill my destiny."

"Mom." Myles broke her reverie. "Mommy. I won't be sad if you won't be sad." Myles reached across the table and squeezed her hand. "It's just the two of us now. Together."

Lenore glowered at her reflection.

***

Earlier that afternoon

Lance Burkett neither saw it nor heard it. The ax swung downward from a tree branch, splitting his sternum. After five seconds of shock at the sight of an ax lodged in his chest, the torment began. "Ahh!" He squeezed his head and stumbled about the glade. Mercifully, losing blood put him in a trance. Homecoming. 1957. Bootleg left. Sprint right for the goal line. Touchdown, Lance Burkett! His teammates lifted him and carried him off of the field. The fans reached up to touch him. He made eye contact with a striking gypsy. "The Gypsy. Green eyes. Green eyes. She was warning me." His lungs filled with corrosive fluid. "Warning me. Why?" Pain returned with a vengeance. His head suddenly felt like an overinflated football, and the kicker was set for a long one. As if an ice pick punctured that football, his breath stormed through his trachea. A volcanic pressure seared against the trauma. He extracted the ax. His entrails erupted. He collapsed onto the ground and tried to stuff his intestines back into his body. He again saw the beautiful and mysterious Gypsy's green eyes. "Why didn't I listen to you?" He steepled his hands. "Oh, God. Oh, Jesus. Wrong. I've been so wrong. Forgive me." Lance felt his brain shatter like an imploding bell jar. All earthly sensations ceased to exist for Lance Burkett.

***

Eric Hildebrandt stepped out of his back door. He scanned the neighborhood in search of a playmate. Nobody. He walked to the next-door field with a Mickey Mantle bat and an old baseball. Tossing the baseball upward, he shifted his hand back to his bat and hit it squarely. He admired the drive's high arc as it disappeared into the woods. Eric entered the woods to look for his ball. He saw something unusual in a glade. 'Comic books…Soaked in blood? It looks like Mr. Burkett.' "Mr. Burkett?" Eric walked closer. Lance's face was colorless. His torso was split open. A rigor mortis grip clutched his intestines. "Ahh!" Eric screamed and covered his face. He whiter than if dipped in flour. He fell to his knees and cried. After five minutes, he uncovered his eyes. The gruesome sight remained. Eric stood and ran home screaming, "Mom! Mom!"

Eric's mother, Mary Hildebrandt, Stanforth's head librarian, ran out the door. "What is it?"

"Blood, Mom, blood! Blood everywhere. In the woods. Mr. Burkett is dead!"

Mrs. Hildebrandt gasped. She put her arm around her son and sat him on the rear porch stoop. Eric buried his face in his hands and sobbed. "Stay right there. I'll call the police."

A riot of sirens and screeching police cars besieged Banjo Town. The entire police force of the township and two neighboring townships arrived with lights flashing and sirens blasting. Dogs could be heard howling at the noise. An ambulance and firetruck had joined them.

The Chief of Yorkshire Township's Police, Michael O'Shaughnessy, stood six-foot-six and weighed over three hundred pounds. He wore a campaign hat with a black strap over the back of his egg-shaped head. He looked at Mrs. Hildebrandt through black, Clark Kent-style glasses. "Mrs. Hildebrandt, I need to talk to your son."

"Okay. Please be gentle. He's traumatized."

"What did you see?" The Police Chief sat next to Eric.

Eric continued to sob into his hands. "Blood. Lots of blood. Mr. Burkett is dead."

"Where exactly?"

"The woods. There's a path. It goes to a clearing. Dead. Mr. Burkett is dead." Eric broke down and bawled.

Chief O'Shaughnessy told the ambulance to go to the path entrance. He walked with two uniformed policemen and a plain-clothed detective.

Officer Abiger puked at the sight of Lance Burkett's butchered corpse. Chief O'Shaughnessy frowned at the rookie cop and then gasped. The paramedic did an initial investigation. "We won't know until the autopsy, but it looks like he's been dead for about four hours. It looks like he was split open with an ax."

"That's my impression." Detective Samuels took several photographs of the crime scene. "The perp took the weapon with him. That will prove our smoking gun."

"I've got bloodhounds on the way from Lower Merion township." Chief O'Shaughnessy adjusted his glasses. "The ax must have left a blood trail. If we can find the ax," the Chief looked at the detective, "I think that we can nip this case in the bud."

***

The bloodhounds barked raucously. They leaped onto the

Burkett's rear door. "No need for a warrant." Chief O'Shaughnessy turned the door handle. "We have exigent circumstances. It's unlocked."

The bloodhounds led the police up the stairs to a linen closet. The dogs leaped on the door. Chief O'Shaughnessy yanked open the door. Geoffrey sat in a daze. His jaw chattered. A bloody ax was next to him."

"Arrest him!" Chief O'Shaughnessy ordered three uniformed policemen.

The policemen brusquely pulled Geoffrey to his feet before slamming him face-first on the floor. Chief O'Shaughnessy cuffed him and read him his rights. The policemen dragged him to an awaiting squad car and drove away with him. Detective Samuels put the ax in an evidence bag.

***

'What's going on?' Lenore's Ford Falcon clunkered into her driveway.

Chief O'Shaughnessy opened her door. "Mrs. Burkett. You better follow me." He led her to a lawn chair. "Please sit."

"What's going on here?"

"This is the hardest part of my job. Mrs. Burkett. It's your husband. He's dead."

"Oh my God." Lenore covered her face. She started to cry while emitting no tears. "What happened?"

"We don't know for sure. All I can tell you is that he died because of foul play."

Lenore uncovered her face. It was void of tears. "You mean, murdered?"

"Yes. I am sorry, Mrs. Burkett. I am afraid it's worse."

"How can this possibly get worse?"

"Our number one suspect is your son Geoffrey. We have taken him into custody."

"I knew he was a bad seed."

Chief O'Shaughnessy blanched at her remark.

Another patrol car pulled into the next-door neighbor's driveway. A policewoman helped Myles out of the car and led him by the hand. He broke free and ran to his mother. "Mommy! I love you." He hugged her. "It's just you and me now. I will help you. I will always be here for you."

Lenore returned his hug.

Chief O'Shaughnessy placed his hands on his hips. "We've done all we can. I am leaving now. For Geoffrey's sake, I don't recommend that you go anywhere, anytime soon. We have much to discuss."

# Chapter 1

A wonderful day for football. Unseasonably warm for a Pennsylvania late November, the sun ruled its azure domain. The weather and publicity attracted hundreds of football fans and sports writers. Their feet crunched on crisp brown leaves as they jockeyed for a better view. They again saw Penn's all-conference lineman, known by all as Hork. Wide receiver Chuck Rankin flanked him. The procession included Sly Horton, Penn's first and finest Black Halfback, Fullback Ted Bodanski, Center Marshall Howard, Defensive end Ed Braceland, and Coach Joseph Samuelson. They broke left, bootlegging their quarterback, Lance Burkett, six feet underground. Melanie Beach Clinton led their tears by waving a black handkerchief over her eyes.

A black-clad Lenore stoically sat by the gravesite. She enjoyed the unexpected attention, but not the sensationalized press over the murder and her murdering older son. Scanning the crowd, she pursed her lips upon failing to find a single Cricket Club member. Myles stood next to her, his head level with his seated mother. He twitched in his custom gray flannel suit, then smiled on overhearing a mourner comment on his adorable looks.

"Ashes to ashes; dust to dust…"

Lenore shook her head. *'Surely the five-thousand-member*

*strong Stanforth Presbyterian church can better that platitude,'*

Afterward, Scotch Sutton led her away by the arm. "I know it looks bad now but have faith. There's no way that Geoffrey murdered Lance. We'll stand together on this. The Suttons have survived tough times before, and this will be no exception."

Lenore looked away. *'No more funeral cliches-- please.'* "How else could it have happened? Please father, I've just lost my husband. Let the police deal with Geoffrey. I also must concern myself with Myles. After all, he lost his father."

Scotch then nodded to Dolly. She took Myles's hand and walked him away. "Lenore, no one needs a PhD in sociology to notice the changes. Ten years ago, those who would've been locked up in a prison or a mental institution now walk the streets. Victims of society, the pundits call them." Scotch scratched the back of his neck. "And the drugs... Any number of people could've done it."

"We live in Stanforth, not in a bad Philadelphia neighborhood."

"I'm so sorry, please accept these with my condolences." A bouquet clenching Pat Huggins stumbled into Lenore and Scotch. The bourbon stench of Pat's breath and tears overmatched the flower's fragrance. "He was, he was…" Lance's best friend broke down.

"He was dear to us all." Scotch steered the sales manager toward the gravesite. "You can best honor him by placing those on his grave. Be careful you don't fall in," Scotch added as Pat staggered away. "Lenore." Scotch looked directly into Lenore's eyes. "I loved Lance as a son, but," Scotch touched his forehead. "How can I say this... Like my real son, your brother Check..."

"Where is Check? I haven't heard from him in days." Lenore lowered her head. "I'm very disappointed, father, that he isn't here."

"I am too. You have done a lot for him. The moment I hear anything from him or about him, I'll call you... This is hard for me to say, but, Lance, like us all, wasn't perfect." Scotch clasped Lenore's shoulder. "I think you know, that his charisma, in addition to attracting friends, made enemies."

Lenore pulled away, saying nothing.

"I'm sorry Lenore." Scotch grabbed her arm. "I guess this isn't the time to talk about it. Look, why don't you and Myles spend some time with us on the farm?"

Lenore stiffened, snapping from her father's grip. "No, no. Please father, I need time alone."

Scotch braced Lenore's shoulders. "Okay. I understand. But if you need anything, at any time, just call."

"Thank you, Father, I will. But please, ultimately this is my burden, and at this time, I think it best I spend some time alone." She tensed her lips and nodded.

Scotch hugged Lenore's unresponsive body, then departed.

* * *

Elizabeth Endicott viewed the proceedings through the one-way window of her Rolls Royce limousine. Noticing that Lenore was finally alone, the society matron again wiped tears from her eyes, then exited without her chauffeur's assistance.

* * *

"Good God." Lenore shut her eyes vise-tight, contorted her lips, and shook her head. '*Sure, my father's words weren't as hackneyed as my in-laws' verbal vapor, but at least they didn't pry.*' Lenore's thoughts shifted to her late husband's parents. Robert and Maxine Burkett. That funeral attire of his. Lenore sniggered on realizing that Bob Burkett had worn the same staid suit to the previous New Year's Eve party. And Maxi. I guess she's too old to grow up and realize that the flappers are out of style. '*You've got to be a football star, if you want to talk to the beautiful girls.*' Memories of Maxi Burkett dancing and singing the old ditty each time she saw her football hero son haunted Lenore. '*At least the Gilby's and Beefeater preserves old Maxi better than the bathtub variety.*' Lenore smirked. '*Go back to your suburban limbo, you two. Live out your lives through memories of Mr. Football. As if you ever had anything better in the first place.* Next, Lenore remembered the big 1957 bowl game. Lance took Marshall Howard's final snap and knelt, killing the closing fourteen seconds. She opened her eyes. Elizabeth Endicott. Instantly Lenore applied her best mourner's face. Yet she felt anger instead of trepidation. "So, you just couldn't wait." The recent widow looked boldly into the committee president's eyes. "Although you make the rules of protocol," Lenore prodded. "I'd think you'd at least wait until my husband is buried before burying me."

"I came not to bury you."

"Well, I'm sure you didn't come to praise me either." Lenore put hands on hips. "Because of my family's poultry farm, your committee never ceased to treat me like a second class citizen. Now my son just created Stanforth's biggest scandal since Benedict Arnold? Now I'm unworthy to even wash dishes at the Cricket Club. Well, I'll save you the trouble…"

Elizabeth held up her hand. "Seeing that we unintentionally cited Shakespeare, I will deliberately quote Wilde, 'Scandal is gossip made tedious by morality.' You don't know this, but, Dolores Preston's husband nearly went to prison for tax violations. Helen Murchenson's son-in-law did serve six months in Shakleford Federal for insider trading. Of course, you do know about Johnny

Kirby and Schiller Sterling. Your friend Janet Boyer has suffered a mental breakdown. Her husband has discreetly committed her to a private sanitarium in Switzerland. He has one of America's top psychiatrists fly out to her once every two weeks."

Lenore dropped her arms and jaw. "When did that happen?"

"Shortly after the New York insurance convention."

"Okay, so I'm not the only one with a few skeletons." Lenore started walking away. "How much more perfect does that make you?"

Elizabeth seized her by the arm. "You don't understand Lenore. I guess you should know. Seeing that I quoted Oscar Wilde."

Lenore's face radiated. "You mean Marion is?"

"Yes, he is." Elizabeth looked directly into Lenore's eyes. "Now do you realize, Lenore, that the Windsor Women's Committee is more than just an elitist social club? I'm afraid we have our shortcomings, just like the rest of society. Even worse, the public often fails to grasp the importance of our mission. Many needy people depend on our efforts. My committee does more for the disadvantaged than any combination of tax funded welfare departments. Unfortunately, some of my members, Dolores and Helen in particular, forget this fact. What I want in a member is someone with intelligence and drive. Janet, of course, is no longer with us. I am promoting Hillary Sterling to her post as committee vice-president. She has the most experience. That still leaves a vacancy at my table. The person that I feel has the intelligence and drive that I'm looking for is," Elizabeth pointed, "You."

The chairwoman's words astounded Lenore like an atheist finding God. "Me? You want me on the committee? Even after I?"

"I considered your ploy to trap Johnny Kirby and Schiller Sterling as quite ingenious."

"But I was…"

"That you were caught will serve to our advantage. Your presence will keep my more complacent members alert."

"But don't the other committee members have to vote me in?"

"You let me worry about them. Meet me at the teak bar on Tuesday morning. I will inform the committee of my decision before you enter." Elizabeth extended her hand.

Lenore's arm jittered forward. Both of Elizabeth's hands clamped Lenore's right hand. Watching Elizabeth walk back to her limousine made Lenore feel twenty pounds lighter. Her astonished mien evolved into a beam.

"Mommy, mommy!" Myles ran toward his mother and embraced her.

Lenore squeezed her son. He secured his head into the small of her back and smiled.

# Chapter 2

The Yorkshire police department had a large bay in the township administration building. Also housed there were the School Board, and the Waste Management, Parks and Recreation, and Fire Departments. A walnut balustrade, extending like two long arms from a reception/charge desk, divided a passage from the policemen's desks. A female radio operator was stationed against the north wall. Two jail cells made up like quaint bed and breakfast chambers were indented into the south wall. The chief of Police had his own office and a six-foot-long desk.

Michael O'Shaughnessy, Yorkshire Township's police chief, wiped the powdery remains of a lemon donut from the corner of his mouth. He also served as a Cub Scout master and Little League baseball commissioner. Early in his career, he mostly gave safety lectures to the township's public, private, and parochial schools, as well as directed traffic at Stanforth's central intersection. His town experienced a spate of tragic accidents and a suicide during the summer of 1961. Over the next eight years, the citizenry increasingly called upon him to break up raucous parties and investigate matters of malicious mischief. Over the last summer and fall, three burglaries and an armed robbery beset the community. Now, for the first time in his twenty-three-year career, he had a homicide. Although the heinous and violent nature of the township's first murder was shocking, the police chief accepted it as inevitable. Chief O'Shaughnessy sighed and reached for a grape-jelly donut. A rapping on his wrist failed to halt the morsel's journey to his mouth.

"Ah, ah, ah, Chief O'Shaughnessy," Psychiatrist Eduardo Tryvye prodded. "You are an anal adult."

"What the?" The police chief nearly dropped his grape-jelly donut.

"Your subconscious mind registered the fact that I ate two grape-jelly donuts. I am consciously cognizant that you prefer lemon and glazed donuts. As an infant, you experienced great anxiety during your potty training sessions. Parental spankings and scoldings abruptly ended your enjoyment of holding onto fecal matter. This manifested into your hoarding and zealously protecting your every toy and possession from your siblings and peers. Now as an adult, this manifests into a compulsion to corner what you subconsciously registered as my favorite: grape-jelly donuts."

Chief O'Shaughnessy looked at the donut with disgust. "Here. You have it." He dumped the donut onto the psychiatrist's plate. "I lost my appetite."

"Do you think I want it now?" Dr. Tryvye flapped his hands. "You already ate off it! Germs, Chief, germs."

"Excuse me, sir. Mrs. Burkett is here." Patrolman D.R. Abiger graduated from preschool tattletale to grammar school belted safety. A former high-school hall monitor, the eighteen-year-old rookie joined the Yorkshire police shortly after receiving his diploma.

"Send her in." Michael O'Shaughnessy, cradling his campaign hat at his side, stood. The chief knew Lenore Sutton long before her romantic attachment to Yorkshire Township's most celebrated athlete. The over 6' 6" tall law enforcement official, nonetheless, personally knew most of his charges.

Lenore's perception of the chief had changed little in twenty years. His size still seemed shielding rather than intimidating. The chief's paunch was still double-barreled. His military buzz-cut hairstyle remained from his police academy days. A thin strap around the back of his egg-shaped head secured the same black Clark Kent glasses.

"Take a seat, Mrs. Burkett." Chief O'Shaughnessy motioned at a chair next to Dr. Tryvye.

Lenore complied.

"Where were you at the time of your husband's murder?" Chief O'Shaughnessy looked into her eyes.

Lenore squirmed. "Um, I've told you before. I was at the

Cricket Club, then I drove home. That juvenile delinquent found his body shortly after I arrived."

"I would hardly call Eric Hildebrandt a juvenile delinquent." Chief O'Shaughnessy adjusted his collar. "He is our respected librarian's son, and he won a scholarship to The Harland School and a sought-after engineering internship at Bechtel Plastics. Your neighbors and his teachers describe him as an All-American boy."

"What-ever. I told you before, any number of witnesses can verify my alibi." Lenore crossed her arms over her waist. "Why must I relive this? You said before that I am not a suspect."

"Your husband was an insurance man, Mrs. Burkett. You did receive a tidy chunk of change from this tragedy. Financially, you are better off without him."

"I beg your pardon!"

The police chief held his hand up. "Just checking, Mrs. Burkett. No, you are not a suspect. The reason I summoned you was to officially close this case."

"Okay. Then how can I help?" Lenore folded her hands on the desk.

"Dr. Tryvye will explain in a moment."

The psychiatrist beamed and nodded to Lenore.

"One more question, Mrs. Burkett," the police chief continued. "We found Geoffrey hiding in a linen closet. When you arrived home, did you suspect that he might be there?"

"No, um," Lenore's eyes rotated wildly. "But he often hid in the closet—whenever he was worried that he might be in trouble. Besides, you greeted me when I arrived home."

"When you can't find him, do you often look for him there?"

"Well, um," Lenore shifted her head back and forth, "When everything is quiet. No reason exists to suspect anything. You greeted me before I could check."

Chief O'Shaughnessy leaned forward. "Did you consider telling me that he might be hiding in the closet?"

"No!" Lenore shook her hands. "When I came home to cop cars, flashing lights, and sirens, I was too upset to think about anything. Call Elizabeth Endicott. She'll tell you that I was at the Cricket Club." Steeling herself, Lenore sat upright. "She's going to nominate me for her committee." After a five-second pause, Lenore raised her chin.

"Yes, of course." Chief O'Shaughnessy sat back. "If not for the Endicotts, I wouldn't be Chief of Police. Okay. Here is what we have. Physical evidence." The chief opened a manila folder. "We found only your son's fingerprints on the murder weapon.

Furthermore, your husband's blood was smeared all over Geoffrey. His possessions, again, covered with only his fingerprints, were scattered about the murder site. Motive. Both your younger son and his friend, Donald, Dr. Frankincense the heart surgeon's son, testified separately, that Geoffrey earlier had attacked the victim with a chair. They both said that Geoffrey lost it on discovering that Lance killed his cat. We didn't find a dead animal. However, the crime lab in Philadelphia did identify blood droplets found in dining room carpet fibers as feline. When last have you seen this cat?"

"Not since the incident," Lenore answered. "But I can tell you that Lance hated cats and that Geoffrey was forbidden to let that animal in the house. So, my husband killing the beast in a fit of rage doesn't surprise me."

"Hmm," Dr. Tryvye gripped his chin. "Ahh," he pointed to the ceiling. "How often did your husband conflagrate into propinquitous fulmination?"

"What?" Lenore curled her lip.

"The rages!" The psychiatrist flapped his hands. "How often did your husband burst into rages?"

"Well, um, often." Lenore lowered her eyes.

"How often?" Chief O'Shaughnessy interjected.

"Look, my husband was a short-tempered man . . ."

"Ya, ya." Dr. Tryvye prodded.

"Hey, what does this have to do with anything?" Lenore raised her palms.

"Need I remind you, that this is a murder investigation?" Chief O'Shaughnessy added.

"All right, all right, if you put it that way ... Mostly when he drank, and especially when he watched his favorite teams lose on television. Look, my husband wasn't a saint. He had a temper. He also drank, gambled, and swore. That still doesn't give Geoffrey the right to split him open with an axe."

"Hmm...Ahh... Mrs. Burkett, we have achieved a realization. A psychiatrist is also a medical doctor. In my physical examination of the boy, I discovered burn trauma on his hand and scalp. A classic manifestation of acute child abuse."

"Well, Mrs. Burkett?" Chief O'Shaughnessy lowered his head toward Lenore. He asserted tight-wire eye contact.

Lenore tugged her collar, then oscillated her head. "My husband, my husband ... in his cruelest moments ... Sometimes punished Geoffrey by putting his hand in the oven flame. My husband," Lenore licked two fingers and kneaded her makeup, "recently poured a cup of hot coffee over his head, after he disturbed him while watching a football game." Lenore squirmed. "Okay, I was married to a monster. Is that a crime?"

"Mrs. Burkett," The police chief stood. "Your husband's actions do indeed constitute a crime. Failure to report or to conceal a crime is also a punishable offense."

"I didn't know ..."

"Ignorance of the law is no defense, Mrs. Burkett."

"It's just that, um, you don't understand. I was a housewife. I depended on my husband to support me and my children. Call it a trap if you like."

"Lenore, I've known you for almost twenty years. You've always impressed me as a strong, independent, and intelligent woman. One who knew what she wanted and knew how to get it. Surely you won't even attempt to tell me that you had to stand for such monstrous abuse to your family." Chief O'Shaughnessy studied Lenore. "And in all these years I've known you, I've never seen any evidence that he physically abused you. Additionally, Myles impresses me as a healthy, active young boy. I doubt very much that your husband abused him. Care to comment?"

"Shouldn't Dr. Tryvye answer that?" Lenore turned to the psychiatrist. Dr. Tryvye deliberately looked forward with a blank face.

After ten tense seconds, she continued: "Look, Chief

O'Shaughnessy, I married Lance Burkett as a starry-eyed college girl. You can't expect me to now analyze him, can you? That's his job." She pointed at the psychiatrist.

He continued to ignore her.

"I want you," the police chief maintained his eye grip on Lenore, "to give it the old college try."

"All right, all right." She held up her hands. "Lance seemed to have this thing against Geoffrey. My husband, as you know, was an acclaimed athlete. A collegiate All-American quarterback. Yet his athletic achievements fell short of professional." Lenore folded her hands palms down on the table. "I think he considered himself a failure for this reason. So, he transferred his athletic aspirations onto his children. Now Myles, he is a warm, affectionate, and well-behaved child. He is also a sports star." Lenore straightened and smiled. "Perhaps you've read about him in the Suburban and Stanforth Times."

"I'm Little League commissioner." Chief O'Shaughnessy nodded. "I know Myles well."

"Yet Geoffrey, he was always sullen and brooding. Antagonistic to family members. And worst of all, to my husband anyway, uncoordinated. Geoffrey hadn't the ability or desire to play sports. Okay. He had an intellectual interest in baseball. His father's least favorite!" Lenore pounded the table. "Now if Geoffrey could've played baseball in your Little League or school team and did well ..." Lenore cupped her chin. "What I'm trying to say is that Lance not only saw him as an extension of his failure to reach his athletic goals but as a rejection of himself. And for this reason ..."

"Hmm," Dr. Tryvye pinched his goatee. "Ahh," he pointed to the ceiling. "Plausible. Plausible. Often a parent will project upon a child their unattainable aspirations. Unfortunately, parents perceiving offspring as falling short of expectations may encounter a vicarious sense of failure. Many times this phenomenon manifests itself in resentment. And of course, rejection. Two ingredients that, sadly, can culminate in violent abuse."

Lenore turned to the psychiatrist. "I've often considered that Geoffrey's devilish traits were inherited from his father."

Dr. Tryvye responded before the police chief could codify Lenore's words. "Hmm…Ahh, a boy's father is a vital agent in his socialization." The psychiatrist pointed to the ceiling. "In my initial examinations of the boy, I determined that he, as all of us, suffered a degree of anxiety manifesting from the stressors of subconscious id versus superego, further battling the conscious cognition of the ego. This manifested in bouts of disruptive behavior, although still within the realm of normalcy. Yet as the acute stressors of Geoff's external environment overwhelmed the tempest of his inner self, his condition deteriorated into an antisocial personality disorder. Geoffrey, furthermore, continually witnessed his father solving his dilemmas and conflicts via the exploitation of violence. That violence was often inflicted on himself. Owing to propinquitous symbiosis, Geoffrey synonymously adopted violence as a solution to his own conflicts. Thus that brutal attack on his schoolmate."

"I'm well aware of that one," Chief O'Shaughnessy interjected. "Bartholomew Hatcher came in here storming and stomping like Rumpelstiltskin, demanding that I send Geoffrey straight to Carlisle State Prison—without trial. Fortunately, Elizabeth Endicott defused the situation by convincing him to drop the charges."

Lenore beamed. "Elizabeth Endicott came up for me?"

"Actually, she came up for Geoffrey," the chief added. "I don't know why. Maybe it's too bad she did. If not, Geoffrey would be in reform school and your husband alive."

Lenore nodded.

"Hmm," Dr. Tryvye rubbed his goatee. "Ahh," he pointed to the ceiling. "We at last have achieved a conclusive insight into the murder of Lance Burkett. His acute abuse of Geoffrey manifested in dual stressors." The psychiatrist held up two fingers. "The first trauma," Dr. Tryvye now sported only his index finger, "that the boy suffered is, of course, emblematic of the external manifestations of his father's violence. The second is predicated on denial," the doctor added his middle finger. "Denial spawned a more serious disturbance. You see, he repressed the pain and humiliation of his father's persecution into his subconscious mind. Although during our sessions he expressed a desire for violent retribution against his father, his free associations excluded the actual severity of his father's violent abuse. This repression transmogrified a borderline personality disorder into an antisocial personality disorder. Now the boy walked the proverbial tight wire between sanity and insanity. Witnessing his father murder his cat pushed him off that wire. You see." The psychiatrist flapped his hands. "His father, by demonstrating murder as a solution, caused Geoffrey, by synonymous extension, to utilize homicide as the ultimate remedy to his own dilemma." Dr. Tryvye beamed, placed his right ankle on his left knee, and folded his hands behind his head.

Lenore looked across at Chief O'Shaughnessy. "Now that the case is solved, I see no need to prolong the matter. Will a protracted trial be necessary?"

"You don't seem very concerned about your son." Chief O'Shaughnessy tilted his head.

"Look. My husband was a monster. That I've established for you. Now Dr. Tryvye has proven that Geoffrey was even worse.

After all, he brutally murdered his father, didn't he? Often, he made my life, and his brother's life, a living hell. Now we know that he is extremely dangerous. Please, Myles and I would just like to start our new lives."

"Don't worry. There won't be a trial. The District Attorney has elected not to press charges."

"What?" Lenore stood and placed her hands on her hips. "Please sit, Mrs. Burkett." Chief O'Shaughnessy pointed.

Lenore sat.

"This county," Chief O'Shaughnessy continued, "is only warranted to try misdemeanors. Felonies fall under the jurisdiction of Philadelphia County. This is only our fifth felony in twenty years, I might add. Let me assure you, Mrs. Burkett, that District Attorney Derrick Anvil is old school. If he could, he would pillory Geoffrey in a town square and allow the citizenry to pelt him to death. Seeing that Geoffrey is only thirteen and without a record, the D.A. realized the impossibility of having him tried as an adult."

"Are you telling me that he'll get off?"

"He will if we try him as a juvenile."

"You're not saying that you won't even try him? Are you?"

"Far worse offenders ..."

"Worse offenders!" Lenore sprung to her feet. "The bastard slew his father with an ax!" She prodded. "What could possibly be worse than that?"

Chief O'Shaughnessy pointed at the chair.

Lenore remained standing.

"Mrs. Burkett, the current social and political climate forces our hand. One fifteen-year-old juvenile delinquent recently murdered and raped an eight-year-old girl. The creep walked with mere probation. Seems because he never knew his father and because his mother was an abusive alcoholic, he wasn't responsible for his actions. Considering that Geoffrey is two years younger, has suffered extreme abuse under his father, and that this cruel father capped it off by killing his little kitty-cat. Well. The bleeding hearts won't just let Geoffrey off with probation ... They'll give him an award."

"But he's dangerous. A murderer! You can't just foist him back on me." Lenore pointed to her chest with both index fingers.

"Hmm...Ahh, Mrs. Burkett. The legal system may be unable to incarcerate your son, but the psychiatric community will protect you, him, and society. A civilian judge and the psychiatric board of Harlond State Mental Hospital have ruled to commit Geoffrey. Sign this," Dr. Tryvye slid a brief with a pen placed atop to Lenore, "and

Geoffrey will not see the outside of Harlond State's walls for a long, long time."

"Fine." Lenore held up the pen. "But doctors are human. Suppose you release him before he's cured. Moreover, seeing that he murdered my husband, you can't just expect me to take him back into my house. You understand that, don't you?"

"Of course, Mrs. Burkett," Chief O'Shaughnessy said. "By signing those papers, you relinquish custody of your son. He becomes a ward of the state."

"You mean?"

"Yes. He will legally cease to be your son."

A smiling Lenore signed.

# Chapter 3

The dimension of time no longer existed for Geoffrey Burkett. Concealed lamps flooded his subterranean cell of glittering white porcelain bricks with ceaseless cold light. The darkness of the Burkett's linen closet at least allowed him sleep. Here he could only restively twitch on a suspended steel bed. A latrine pan was welded to the wall of his windowless cage. Yet most of the ward's prisoners used their cell floor's center drain. In the quiet privacy of his closet, Geoffrey could transcend himself to extraterrestrial worlds. And George? No more ghostly visits. At Harland State, the company often broke his reveries.

"Sex, blood, death, Satan's way is best! Sex, blood, death, Satan's way is best!" A madman in the adjacent cell broke the incessant hum of the ward's ventilation system.

Geoffrey covered his ears, squeezing away the incantation. How he longed for the musty odor of mildewed towels. For covering his ears exposed his nose to the ever-present urine and fecal stench. Yet the malodorous place smelled worse than sewage. An evil seemed to steep its stale air. Often his Lee Lee cat joined him in the closet. Here only hunger and boredom accompanied him. Thoughts of his friend Norman, George the ghost, and tears for Yogi and Lee Lee filled his confinements few undisturbed moments.

Two burly orderlies entered a cell. "Ahh! No! Ahh!" The patient scrunched into a fetal position. Viciously rubber hoses splayed his body like the tentacles of a farm thrasher. Geoffrey, sitting on his bed's edge, slumped over and covered his eyes. More than not wanting to watch the ghastly spectacle in the cage across the hall, making eye contact with the perpetrators could invite similar punishment.

"Death and night and blood, fuck God's love." The madman continued to yell. Geoff soon realized that this inmate terrified even the guards. A skinny thirteen-year-old boy, however, posed no such threat to the orderlies. Fortunately, he still hadn't received a beating, but the guards always expressed their contempt for him.

"Guess we gotta slop the father killer." An orderly slid a tin plate of cold beans and two slices of stale bread under his cell door.

Geoff steepled his fingers, closed his eyes, and silently moved his lips.

"Ah, ah, ah," Dr. Tryvye interrupted Geoff's prayer. "What did we say about that?"

"Jesus knows I didn't kill my father. He will save me."

"Only you can save yourself. And I decide when that happens." Dr. Tryvye nodded to two guards. They opened his cell, leaving the door ajar. The psychiatrist entered.

"You don't understand. The holy spirit is here with me. Apostle Paul and Silas..."

"Did we not analyze a historical paradigm?" Dr. Tryvye rapped the boy's knuckles. "The Hebrews murdered Moses. Remorse over their homicidal transgression stimulated their fantasy of a Messiah. One who would return and redeem their nefarious deed. Your behavior confirms this paradigm. Inventing a similar ethereal savior poses an analogous manifestation of your repressed remorse manifesting from patricide. Hmm, ahh."

"The Hebrews did not! And Jesus is real. He loves me," Geoffrey tapped his chest, "I can feel it. He's right here with me."

"Hmm," Dr. Tryvye pinched his chin. "Ahh," he pointed to the ceiling. "The prattle of an inerudite mind."

"It's not about the mind. It's about the heart."

"No. It is about the mind, and you're afflicted by an illusion of the mind. That you will have to reconcile before I permit you to leave. Your father is dead."

"But Jesus lives."

"Ah, ah, ah," Dr. Tryvye rapped Geoffrey's wrist. "In here we will not discuss illusions as if they were tangible facts. Your father is dead. That is a fact, a material reality; is it not? Do you not mourn for him?"

"I mourn for Lee Lee."

"Ahh, your cat. Did you presume murdering your father would manifest into the resurrection of your fallen pet? Well, your father is dead. Your cat remains dead. And you are here. Until you face the reality of your actions, here you will remain."

"On the Lamb's blood, Lucifer will feast! Hail to the beast!" the madman yelled.

"What makes you think your beliefs are any saner than his?" the psychiatrist asked.

"Because Jesus is about love and truth. The Devil is lies and hate."

"Well, you better believe this, save a weekly shower, he hasn't been out of his cell," Dr. Tryvye pointed to the madman's cage, "since before your birth. How long do you wish to remain in this cell? You were acquitted of all criminal charges. Harlond State Mental Hospital is a place of treatment, not punishment. If you will cooperate and tell the truth about your father, we will move you to a real room. With a real bed. Carpets. A window. Better food. If your behavior manifests a measurable degree of improvement, we will even let you play outside. Harland State has beautiful grounds."

"I told you the truth. I didn't kill my father. Jesus knows I didn't."

"But does Santa Claus?" The psychiatrist scornfully laughed. "Christmas draws nigh. Patricide will most surely manifest in a stocking full of coal."

"One, two, three, four, Christ is the son of a fucking whore!" the madman shouted.

"My friend Norman ... He told me, that, long ago, Jesus conquered the Devil. He exists only on borrowed time. At the end, God will bind Satan in chains and toss him into the lake of fire for eternity."

Dr. Tryvye nodded to two brawny orderlies. They ran in and pinned Geoff face first to the porcelain floor. The psychiatrist pulled a syringe from his leather portfolio and spiked Geoff's right butt-cheek. The boy twitched before losing consciousness.

# Chapter 4

The Windsor Cricket Club Women's Committee.

"Do you know what I heard, really happened to Janet?" Dolores Preston murmured to Helen Muchenson.

"You're kidding!" Helen clutched Dolores's arm. "The same thing happened to Jennifer on Ann Walt Place."

"It's too bad about Janet," Betty interjected. "I'm curious to hear what she'd say about the now," Betty paused for effect, *Miss* Chicken Farm and her family."

"I remember two years ago Jack Ryant poisoned Jennifer's husband." Helen sipped a dry Martini. "Well, they never did reveal who did it. But I just know it was ... Ugh ... Him. Who else could it have been? After all, he seduced Jennifer right after. Then he ... Ugh ... Dumped her. That's why she had a breakdown. But to murder your father. Even *he* never did that."

"Ironic, isn't it." Betty twittered her fingers. "The only reason that she got her man, took her man. Te, he, he," Betty giggled. "What goes around, comes around.   Boy, isn't that the truth."

"Well," Hillary sat upright and folded her hands on the table. "Elizabeth has a special announcement to make. I can't tell you what it will be. But I can assure you, that our table will now be reserved for only…"

Elizabeth Endicott entered.

The committee members silenced and straightened their seating posture.

Elizabeth nodded to Martin. He hustled over and pulled her Throne. Elizabeth sat, placing several briefs before her. "Thank you for your reticence and punctuality. I have two important announcements to make before we discuss final arrangements for our Thanksgiving banquet. Janet Boyer, as you probably heard, resigned her committee seat to oversee her family's European business concerns."

Betty and Hillary pulled their faces and nodded to each other.

"Janet's departure creates a double void. The first is Woman's Committee Vice-president. Our new Vice-president shall be," Elizabeth, fingers steepled, achieved eye contact with all four underlings. "Hillary Sterling."

Hillary stood and raised her chin.

Elizabeth clapped. Betty, Helen, and Dolores followed. The committee president then nodded to her new vice president. She sat. "Janet's departure, of course, creates a vacant committee seat. I've chosen a new approach in nominating our newest member," Mrs.

Endicott continued. "Normally, familial pedigree takes precedence in judging our candidates, and for good reason. The Windsor Cricket Club Women's Committee has always spearheaded the bearing and protocol of refined society. Yet refined society can only neglect the public at her peril. Need I mention the French and Russian revolutions as two of many examples? In the past, the public revered the committee. The disadvantaged looked upon us as their primary source of succor. Now scorn and contempt often mark the community's attitude toward us and our goodwill, allowing government departments to usurp our objectives. The only way to reverse this trend," Elizabeth rapped the table, "is to intensify our charitable endeavors. I have therefore chosen the candidate most capable of augmenting the efficacy of our calling. My selection commands that needed drive and intelligence. Those are the components, I expect each of you, as duty-bound committee members, to judge." The committee president nodded to Martin. He opened the door. Lenore entered.

Helen covered her heart and gasped; Dolores ticced her head; Hillary stood and pointed at Elizabeth. The new Vice-president's lips silently quavered her protests. Suddenly Betty Kirby stood and stormed out of the room. "Bam!" She slammed the door.

"Sit!" Mrs. Endicott growled and pointed at Hillary's seat. She promptly sat. "Not one of you," Elizabeth continued, "no, not anyone here, is irreplaceable. If any one of you, is unhappy, with any of my decisions, then, thank you very much, you may turn in your seat. Never has the Windsor Cricket Club Woman's Committee lost more civic standing than this past year. That is going to end. If I must effect personnel changes, I will. Betty Kirby reacted in a most unbecoming manner. Hillary," Elizabeth lowered her forehead and aimed her steepled fingers. "Your first assignment as committee Vice-president shall be to admonish her. Inform her that another such outburst will result in her dismissal from the committee. You will make that perfectly clear. Understood?"

Hillary timidly nodded.

"All in favor of admitting Lenore Burkett to the committee say yea." One by one, Elizabeth, like a truant officer confronting the dead-end kids, bore into the eyes of her minions.

"Yea," the committee squeaked.

"Excellent. To further advance the committee's status with the community, we need a youth outreach. Times have changed and the changes are accelerating. Many would argue not for the better. That is irrelevant. Either we change with the times or our function will become obsolete. I have there for placed my daughter Estelle in charge of forming a youth committee that will work directly under us. My daughter has the necessary intelligence, strength of character, and maturity to make it a success." Elizabeth then made individual eye contact with each of the committee members. She paused so that they could applaud. After a few seconds, Elizabeth held up her hand. They silenced. "Next on the agenda is the Thanksgiving banquet." Elizabeth sorted several briefs. "Each year Windsor's Thanksgiving banquet ranks among the highlights of the social calendar. I expect this year's event to be newsworthy. The Kersey Children's Hospital depends on it. Windsor's invitees will, of course, enjoy a traditional turkey feast at home with their families. Nonetheless, our two hundred dollars-a-plate dinner is expected to uphold the historic integrity of the holiday, yet still provide a variation from the season's turkey saturation. We are therefore serving roast goose with wild rice and brandied apples. Rightly, Argus Brothers are providing the provisions." Elizabeth folded her hands on the table and looked forward. "Yet I am most delighted to announce, that I have obtained the services of Billy White Eagle. The nation's foremost chef specializing in traditional American dishes." The committee president paused. She continued after her acolytes clapped. "A chamber group from the Philadelphia Orchestra will entertain. I cannot deem the event a success, however, unless my guests donate an additional twenty thousand dollars to The Kersey Children's Hospital. Hillary, I placed you in charge of the decor. What can you report?"

"Well, um, in addition to the customary seasonal decorations, I have contacted various museums in Plymouth Massachusetts and Williamsburg Virginia. They agreed to lend us several genuine artifacts of the Indians and European settlers. Betty and I are planning a display ..."

"Betty Kirby is dismissed from your subcommittee."

"What?" Hillary dropped her jaw.

"Seeing that Betty Kirby doesn't deem this meeting as worthy of her presence, she forfeits the privilege of participating in my event. Her replacement is Lenore Burkett."

Lenore beamed.

"But Elizabeth!" Hillary stood and pointed at the Committee President.

Mrs. Endicott calmly looked at another underling. "Dolores. Since Mrs. Sterling has a problem with ..."

"No. No." Hillary held up her hands and sat. "I'll happily work with Mrs. Burkett. I promise we'll make the decor for this year's gala most memorable."

"Very well.  I trust you to keep your word. Our next meeting is not until after the Thanksgiving Banquet. Until then I want each of you to ponder ideas for our Christmas functions.

Proactive thinking can only enhance our preparations. Meeting adjourned." Elizabeth gathered her documents, stood, and departed in her best coronation gait.

Lenore flounced from the room. Helen and Dolores murmured to each other before leaving.

Hillary remained. Jaw agape, she stared at the wall.

* * *

"Oh doll, I'm sorry. I'm so very sorry." Martin caught Lenore by the arm. "Martin! The most wonder ..."

"The right words are so hard to find." Martin placed is hand over his heart. "But you do have my sincerest and deepest condolences. I never met your husband, but my close friend Marion has. He only met him once, but he raved about him. An inspiration, a true inspiration. Right afterward he sculpted Hercules. Elizabeth wants the school district to establish an annual Lance Burkett award for their best athlete. And what Elizabeth Endicott wants, Elizabeth Endicott gets. Marion is already fashioning the trophy. It will outclass even the Heisman."

"You don't understand. I'm on the committee!" Lenore quaked like a schoolgirl announcing her prom date. "Elizabeth Endicott named me to her committee."

Lenore's attitude thunderstruck Martin.

"They won't ever again dare, utter the word chicken farm. Now I'm one of them. And no one can take that away from me."

"Well, um, there is one who can, and she summons."

"What?" Lenore placed hands on hips.

"Over there." Martin pointed to the teak bar. Elizabeth Endicott beckoned for Lenore. She froze.

"You best not keep her waiting." Martin directed Lenore toward the teak bar. Flummoxed, he shook his head as she gingerly heeded the society matron's call.

*　*　*

"Bloody Mary?" Elizabeth asked.

"Um, yes please," Lenore bit her left pinky finger.

Mrs. Endicott nodded to the bartender.

He pulled a Vodka bottle from the top shelf.

The society matron held up her hand and shook her head.

The black-tied bartender replaced the bottle. He then opened a strong box and grasped a six-inch long brass key. Soon he returned from a back room carrying a bottle with a Russian-lettered label.

"Oh, it's Lenore Burkett. Scotch Sutton's daughter." Clad in purple sox, polka dot knickers, and a baby blue cardigan, the sixty-year-old Walden Paper heir placed his green golf hat on the bar. "Clarkson Merideth Walden IV." Golden putter on shoulder, he extended his right hand. "You can call me Clark."

Lenore limply shook his hand.

"Scotch Sutton. Great Lawyer. Among the best," Clark said to Elizabeth. "The next time you see your father," the heir turned to Lenore. "Tell him that if he ever tires of those clucking chickens, to give me a call. I've got a healthy retainer waiting for him."

Lenore flushed and lowered her head. "Lenore is my newest committee member," Elizabeth said to Clark.

"Congratulations." Clark leaned his putter on the teak bar and cupped Lenore's right hand with two hands. "I'm just an old golf bum. But the Women's Committee *is* the Windsor Cricket Club. If you're half as clever as your father, I'm sure you'll prove a great asset."

"She will. I'm counting on it," Elizabeth interjected. "Lenore. Someone else I want you to meet."

Lenore turned in the direction of Mrs. Endicott's gaze. The recent widow's eyes opened wider than a rookie soldier's at the first sight of a rocket's red glare.

Shoulders comfortably wider than hips, the six-foot-tall, fifty-year-old man's full head of hair boasted a perfect match of salt and pepper. He wore sockless Navona loafers, Ferragamo slacks, and a MacGregor turtleneck shirt. Black Rayban Sunglasses were tucked into the breast pocket of his Armani blazer.

"Lenore. Introducing Lawrence Wainwright Madison V. Windsor Cricket Club's president." Elizabeth linked the gentleman and Lenore by grasping each of their arms.

"Oh, come on Liz ..."

Hearing the gentleman address the society matron with a chummy nickname caused Lenore to double-take.

"Lawrence Wainwright Madison V." He chuckled and turned to Lenore. "I bet you think the Cricket Club's register has more Roman numerals than Cicero's census. Wayne will suffice." The gentleman braced Lenore's shoulder as he shook her hand.

"Lenore." Lenore's eyes opened wide. Her jaw dropped.

"Don't worry Lenore. I don't bite." He chuckled and turned to the Woman's Committee president. "Even if I did, it wouldn't hurt. I'm just a paper tiger around here. Liz here bares the teeth."

Before Elizabeth could respond, Martin interjected. "Mrs. Endicott, so sorry to interrupt.

Janet Boyer's psychia...I mean, Dr. Tryvye, wants you to call him right away."

"Thank you, Martin. I'll phone him from my office." Elizabeth turned to the gentleman. "You'll have to please excuse me." Chin raised, she departed.

"To tell the truth, Lenore, I'm glad to have you alone." Wayne gently placed his hand over Lenore's, regaining her attention. "The other members mean well, of course. That I'm sure you appreciate, even when their stilted clichés do make you feel worse instead of better. But only the two of us," Wayne braced Lenore's shoulders, "who actually are grieving the sudden loss of a beloved mate, can truly understand."

"Yes, um . . ."

"I'm sorry Lenore. You must still be in shock. The first two days after losing Dorothy, I felt numb as if my soul were receiving Novocain intravenously. For days afterward, I simply denied it. It couldn't be. How could it be?" Wayne squeezed Lenore's hand. "On a Tuesday morning, she sees our family G.P. for a routine mammogram. He finds a small lump and assures us it's benign. The next day a specialist performs, what they promised would be a simple operation. So basic, the surgeon assured Dorothy she'd spend only one night in the hospital, just for observation. Then...then," Wayne pinched the bridge of his aristocratic nose and dropped his rectangular head. "When he told me she suffered heart failure, I felt as if some entity ripped my soul from my body. I could virtually see myself from another dimension. Unfortunately, a different dimension from Dorothy." Wayne took both of Lenore's hands. "I know that you've heard everything, but not only have I experienced it: I'm still living it. I'm here for you Lenore; I am."

Flabbergasted, Lenore's jaw chattered as she ducked from the gaze of his hazel eyes. "Um, um, I don't know what to say."

"Say nothing. I understand." Wayne reasserted his grip to Lenore's shoulders. "Depression and despair are indulgences, a faux pas of life that I command the will to resist. Anger, unfortunately, sometimes possesses me." Wayne shook both fists. "Fury directed sometimes at no one in particular. The doctors? God? What possible plan for the good could conceivably exclude my Dorothy? Not just from me, but from humanity."

"She was Women's committee president, wasn't she?" Lenore asked.

"In name only. Actually, she was Liz's lieutenant. And that's the way Dorothy wanted it. You see, Lenore, my wife wasn't a woman of ambition or conceit. She genuinely believed in the committee's calling to the disadvantaged. Dorothy realized that Elizabeth Endicott was the mover and shaker, an organizer and field general second to none. I sometimes feel Liz gets a bit carried away with that. Yet Dorothy," Wayne folded his arms on the teak bar.

"She gave the committee its heart. The poor saw her as not just a source of financial succor, but as a true fountain of love and compassion."

"Yes." Lenore mustered the courage to look into his misty eyes. "The news of Dorothy's untimely passing saddened me deeply."

"Thank you, Lenore." Wayne tapped Lenore's hand. "I appreciate your indulging a lonely man. I know a time of understanding and acceptance will someday arrive. I know you've also heard that enough over the past few days to make you sick. Nevertheless, that time will come for you too. I never had the opportunity of actually meeting your husband, but as a Penn alumni, I often cheered for him from Franklin Field's Poor Richard Box. If ever I adopted a younger man as a hero, it was Lance Burkett. Lenore," Wayne cradled both of Lenore's hands. "Idolatry and ancestor worship are unbecoming of us as civilized human beings. True. I'll never again find someone with Dorothy's exact qualities. Although I do know that others possess different, yet equally noble traits. That Dorothy always believed. Lenore," Wayne opened his eyes wide while arching his eyebrows. "Men who can boast Lance's heroic, masculinity are rarer than Javan Tigers. Yet men can be heroes in many ways. Look at others this way and you will again find happiness. That I promise."

Lenore's pupils dilated as she beheld the distinguished character of Wayne's face. Something deeper than a young Lance Burkett's model Teutonic visage affected her. Although not taut as the quarterback's skin, the gentle lines of Wayne's face harmonized with his rounded cheekbones. Her expression broadened. She recalled Penn's 1957 homecoming ball. A debutante Betty Kirby cringed as Lenore proudly entered on the man of the hour's arm. Brusquely, images of their Banjo Town hovel and Betty Kirby's surgically trimmed snout curled Lenore's lip.

Wayne clasped her hand.

She felt his reach levitate her. Below, Betty Kirby and Hillary Sterling, confined to a pit, flailed their arms and hands to her. Rising higher, Wayne Madison's hand pulled her to the clouds. Lenore saw Betty and Hillary dissolve into a teeming mass of snake-entwined, condemned souls. Abruptly Lenore's fantasy put her next to Lance's maggot-eaten corpse's grave. "Thud!" Geoffery, Betty, and Hillary shoveled dirt on her face. Lance's best friend, Pat Huggins, poured bourbon from a brown paper-bagged bottle into her stinging eyes. Eddie Krause and Paul Barton slung misogynist epithets ..."What's wrong? What's wrong." Wayne shook an ashen Lenore.

"I'm sorry Wayne. It's just that, well," Lenore dropped her head. "Dorothy died of natural causes. But my husband ..."

"Lenore." Wayne squeezed her shoulders. "You must not be ashamed of, or angry at, Geoffrey. Blue blood. What ignoramus posed that an aristocrat's blood is hued in anything but the crimson of the common man?" He pounded the bar counter. "Yes, I was a millionaire at four years of age. Yes, both Dorothy and I trace our lineage to the Mayflower. Yet does that make us genetically superior? Geoffrey?" Wayne lowered his head. "I understand. In the worst possible way, I understand. You see, my daughter, well, um ... Let's not talk here." He stood and pulled Lenore by the hand. "Come. I want to take you to a special place."

* * *

Lenore and Wayne sat on a sculpted wrought iron bench. Above arched a vine clad Carrara marble gazebo. "You probably thought secret gardens existed only in romantic fiction. Yet here we are. Many members of the Cricket Club don't even know this spot exists, much less visited it."

"How can this, this piece of heaven, ever remain secret?" An awestruck Lenore scanned the private grotto. It was walled in the renaissance tradition of Villa Gamberaia near Florence.

"Shh." Wayne put finger before bunched lips. "A traitor selling Operation Overlord to the Nazis, would've gotten more mercy from the military, than anyone revealing this place will from

Elizabeth Endicott. Actually, I'm ashamed. Ashamed that here, and only here, in this secret of secret sites, will I discuss Karen. My only daughter. Lenore." He turned and grasped her hands. "Karen has autistic disorder. No one really knows what causes it. The specialists say it's a birth defect. Yet even they're unsure As an infant, Karen was so unresponsive that Dorothy and I once suspected she was deaf"

"Hmmm . . ." Lenore pinched her chin. "Geoffrey's condition was never that serious. Unfortunately, he would only arbitrarily mind us, and even then, so briefly, that we also thought he might've had a hearing problem." Lenore lowered her head. "Even as disorderly and disruptive a child as he was, I never suspected that he could've, could've ... Oh Wayne, I tried so hard." Lenore shook her fists. "I gave him so much love, kindness, and attention." She started sobbing. "I ask myself: what could I have done differently? But I honestly can't imagine that I could've been a more prefect, loving parent. But he, but he ..."

"It's O.K. Lenore." Wayne embraced a wailing Lenore, patting her back. "I understand. I understand. Come." He stood and extended his hand.

She obliged.

He helped her to his feet. "Ironic, isn't it?" Hand in hand

Wayne walked with Lenore. "Here I walk through this private paradise, bemoaning to you Karen's condition, the worst of which is that she retreats into her own world. For hours on end she'll dazedly rock back in forth in front of the T.V., and just when I think she's lost in her imaginary wonderland, she'll lash out at me, Dorothy, or anyone present. I guess only here, in my own hidden wonderland, surrounded by such pure beauty, can I gain any understanding. Plato, after all, said: 'If there are arts, there is a standard of measure, and if there is a standard of measure, there are arts, but if either is wanting, there is neither'."

"What do you think Plato meant?" Lenore asked.

"That via art, not only can we make an objective judgment as to what is beautiful, but also gain an insight into the human soul. In times of sorrow and anguish, I find solace by absorbing the beauty and passion of fine art. I guess that's how I reconcile myself to life. Lenore, whenever I walk these parterres, admiring the Vignola fountains, Lachaise columns ..."

"And these marble statues," Lenore interjected. "They are, they are, magnificent." She turned to Wayne, inching closer to him. "They take my breath away. Literally. I'm no expert," she held out her palms to him, "but I can't imagine more ideal male bodies. Really Wayne, they're so individual while staying in such perfect proportion. They put me under a spell. How did the Cricket Club ever unearth such masterpieces?"

Wayne grinned foxlike. "Easily. Elizabeth Endicott's son sculpted then."

"Figures." Lenore chortled. "I know for a fact that he's ..."

"Shh." Wayne placed a finger before bunched lips. "That you must never mention. Don't judge him for anything other than his art. After all, Lenore, doesn't art often embody its creators and their times to reveal enduring truths about the human condition? Call me old fashioned, Lenore, but the art, music, and poetry of our present time's madness and destruction too often debases and profanes."

"Rather like the Cole Porter song," Lenore added. "Authors who once knew better words, now only use four-letter words. Heaven knows, anything goes," she chortled.

Wayne also chuckled. ''Now you know why I so appreciate Marion Endicott's work. Does it not bridge us to a time when mankind strived for a higher order of civility?"

"I guess it doesn't matter that he's ..."

Wayne held up his hand. "A love and appreciation for physical beauty softens our hearts. It grants us the capacity for mercy and compassion. Let Marion Endicott be. Never should anyone hinder his creativity. How much poorer would we as a civilization be, for example, if the Sistine Chapel were painted flat white, with a roller?" Lenore and Wayne both chuckled.

"You see. I'm laughing. I'm actually laughing." Wayne shook his hands. "The artistic and natural beauty of this wonderful garden truly is redemptive." He raised his nose, smelling roses growing in a small greenhouse. "Although the whys for Karen's condition and Dorothy's death may forever baffle me, here, surrounded by all of this." He waved his right arm. "I can say: farewell bitterness."

"Thank you, Wayne. Thank you so much for sharing this garden with me. You're helping me realize just how lucky I am. My other son. Myles. He's been wonderful. Just wonderful throughout the whole ordeal. Despite the loss of a husband, and for all intents and purposes, a son, we've become a true family."

"I'm glad to hear you say that. I truly am. Unfortunately, I'm still undergoing a fierce tribulation. A battle within my very soul. Dorothy. She gave Karen more love than any ten parents could give a child. Sadly, that child usually didn't acknowledge that source of unconditional love. Nevertheless, a beacon of optimism and hope Dorothy remained 'till the end. If only I could muster half her positive spirit, but each time I do, reality slugs me in the gut." Wayne lowered and shook his head. "Even if Karen does miraculously emerge from her state, her low IQ will always hinder her. I'm ashamed to tell you this Lenore, but I can no longer handle her by myself Her condition leaves me with no other option besides an institution. No, not Harlond State, but a home. Somewhere peaceful. With attendants that can give her the professional care she requires."

"Like where Janet Boyer is."

"That's another thing you must never discuss." Lenore turned pallid. "It's O.K. Lenore." Wayne patted Lenore's arm. "We can talk about anything here. That's why I brought you."

Lenore sighed in relief "Thank you Wayne. Thank you for bringing me. As lovely as it is now, I wish I could picture its beauty in spring and summer, when its flowers are in full bloom."

Wayne grinned. "Splendid in spring and summer indeed. Yet late November gives us a deeper insight into the virtuosity of this garden's design. First, consider classical art's symmetry and order, then consider Pennsylvania's unique balance of the four seasons. In Spring, this garden's pink blossoms soon lead to Summer's florid bloom of blazing saffron, vermilion, and blue aubrietia. Geraniums, daisies, zinnias, marigolds, lilies, and orchids then flower abundantly. Green will conceal the garden's walls, arches, and balustrades. Green that turns chromatic in fall, soon swaying to winter's stalactite ice veil."

"You say that so poetically." A wide-eyed Lenore spoke in her highest octave.

Wayne chuckled. "Thank you for saying that. Unfortunately, most call it magniloquence. Poetry, as William Wordsworth put it, 'is the spontaneous overflow of powerful feelings. It takes its origin from emotion recollected in tranquility. I'd like to bring you here and read you my favorite verses."

Lenore's pupils dilated as if capturing a bead of light in a dark tunnel. "You read poetry?

Lance never read anything besides the sports page."

"Believe it or not, I always considered the athletics of Lance Burkett on the gridiron as a form of poetry. Poetry in motion so to speak. Much like a ballerina's artistic grace."

"I can't imagine Lance in a pink tutu." Lenore guffawed.

"Lance Burkett, Lance Burkett ... In a pink tutu! Ha! Ha! Ha!" Wayne guffawed. "Come, come." Attempting to compose himself, Wayne extended his hand. "We've just about reached my favorite spot in the garden." Wayne lead Lenore to a brilliant green, hog-backed wooden footbridge. The simple span, arching over a rocky stream, sported no supporting piers. They stood at its apogee.

"This bridge," Lenore asked, "is Japanese, isn't it?"

"Sort of It's patterned after the footbridge in Claude Monet's own secret garden in Givemy France. He designed it after a Japanese print hanging in his dining room. In summer, this bridge's trellises support racemes of blue, white, pink, and purple flowers. Nevertheless, what late November lacks in sight and scent, she more than compensates in sound. This trout stream, originating from that water stairway," Wayne pointed to a large fountain which once centered a town square in Canterbury England, "unfettered by spring and summer's white, yellow, mauve, and rose waterlilies, and of course, winter's ice, can now flow freely. Listen to it buffet against its stones."

"Yes. I see, I mean, I hear what you mean. Marvelous." Lenore bent over the balustrade and gazed into the stream. "This stream. Yes. You're right. It chirps like a songbird."

"Soothing. Isn't it?"

"Yes. Yes. Very much so." Lenore's eyes met Wayne's.

"And the walls, as I wanted to say before," Wayne placed his hands on her shoulders, "only in late November when freed from summer's vines and winter's ice, can one appreciate the crystalline starkness of its quartz and limestone."

"Yes. November. The quartz. The limestone. It's beautiful." Lenore kept her widening pupils fixed on Wayne.

He then touched her cheek. She tingled as his fingertips warmed her cold flesh.

The mineral austerity of Lenore's features affected Wayne strangely. Her eyes shone like the wall's glistening stones. Their heads gradually approached, like docking spacecraft. Silently, they kissed. Their tongues mingled as the frigid stream below beat a lub-dub cadence over its rocks.

# Chapter 5

Norman rubbed his hands over a fire in a trash can. "Sure could use a fur coat like yours," he said to a Siamese cat.

"Meow." The cat buffed a figure eight against his ankles.

"That all you got to say?" He lifted the feline before his nose. "And you can't play checkers either. That ain't too bad I guess. You also don't complain."

Suddenly Sasha voiced an alarm of staccato mews.

Norman released the Siamese and hopped into his shack. He scrunched against a wall, beside the splintery front door. Warily he peaked through a crack. "Lord have mercy!" He flung open the door. "A human gets just one life here, then another hereafter. I don't know what you get hereafter, but you've used up eight of your earthly lives, that's fa-sure." The hobbling white cat collapsed. Norman gently lifted and cradled her. He detected that three of her ribs were broken. Dried blood, mud, and tangled weeds caked her fur. "But don't you worry. We're gonna make your ninth life a long one." He tucked the injured cat into a moth-eaten blanket atop his bed and wrapped an old rag around her torso. Next, he mixed a bowl of ripple, powdered milk, and oatmeal. The cat painfully slurped her first sustenance in days. Afterward, she slept deeply. Lee Lee had begun her recovery.

# Chapter 6

"Sophie, make sure you serve dinner on the old plates ... Not the new china."

"Yes, Mrs. Burkett," the fifty-eight-year-old maid answered in a heavy Eastern European accent. "But don't you want me to serve the goulash from your new tureen?"

"That would be nice," Lenore answered.

"Let me get it." Barging to the kitchen, Myles bumped the blue uniformed, curly black-haired servant aside. Seconds later, he returned with a large copper pot. "Here mommy." He put it on the table then scooted over to an antique cupboard. The brat grabbed a white bowl with a yellow floral motif and placed it before his mother. "One or two scoops, mommy?" He poured a ladle of stew into her dish.

"That's enough, thank you." Lenore held up her hand. "But honey. That's Sophie's job."

"No mommy. You gotta let me do it." Myles returned to his seat and dished himself a serving. "Yesterday the teacher sent me to the guidance counselor. She asked how I was doing. You know, if I was sad and all about daddy. I said no. I have to be brave for my mommy."

"Awww ... That's sweet of you honey."

The maid watched the scene with hands on hip.

"Oh, Sophie. I noticed the brass kitchen cabinet handles are starting to tarnish. Don't you want to polish them now?"

"Yes Mrs. Burkett."

"And while you're at it, rub some lemon oil into the oak."

"Yes Ma'am. I'll take care of it right away." En route to the kitchen, Sophie tried to ignore Myles's scowl.

Myles slurped some goulash. "Uww ... This stinks. You should let me make dinner for you mommy. I can do it. Give me a chance. Please?"

"Maybe later. You're right. This doesn't look too appetizing, does it?" Lenore draped a white linen napkin over her bowl. "I'm going out for dinner tonight anyway. But you need to eat yours now, if you want to grow up into a big, strong football player."

"What? You're going out to dinner?" Myles's voice raised as his jaw dropped. "Yes, Myles. Sophie will take care of you. You be nice and do what she says."

"But Mawww ..."

A rapping on the door interrupted Myles.

"Oh, he must be here early." Lenore's eyes raised. "He?" Gravy dribbled to the brat's chin.

Smiling, Lenore glided to the front door and opened it. "Oh," she moaned. "Well, that's the strangest . . ."

"Grand-dad!" Myles ran toward Scotch Sutton.

"Well, how's my boy? Uhh," he groaned as he lifted Myles. "Are you getting big!"

"That's cause I'm a big boy now. I gotta be a man, for mommy."

"So you're helping your mother around the house?"

"Oh yes, Granddad! All the time."

"Well, that's a good boy." Scotch put Myles down then patted his head.

Lenore smiled. "Yes, he's been wonderful. And Myles, why don't you keep being a good boy and go inside and eat all your dinner." Myles obeyed.

Suddenly she sharpened her aquiline mien and closed the door. "What are you doing here? You didn't even call."

"What am I doing here?" Scotch crossed his arms. "Since when do I need an appointment to visit my daughter?"

"I'm sorry. I didn't mean it that way. It's just that, well, considering what has happened, the last thing I need is more surprises."

"I understand that, Lenore. But what I have to say can't wait. Your son ..."

"Myles is doing just fine. I don't know what I'd do without him."

"No. Geoffrey."

"Geoffrey!" Lenore turned her back on Scotch and started opening the front door. "If you came to talk about him, then consider your visit over."

Scotch clutched Lenore's arm. "Geoffrey's innocent. I know it. You must have faith. In the meanwhile ..."

"Innocent?" Lenore put hands on hips and jutted her jaw. "Look. You never had to live with him. I did. And it was damn near impossible. Among other things, he terrorized his younger brother. His bullying recently put a schoolmate in the hospital. That misdeed put him within a cat's whisker of expulsion-- and maybe even reform school. Myles and his friend Donald, Dr. Frankincense's son, both testified-- separately-- to seeing Geoffrey attack his father with a chair. And that's just the circumstantial evidence. The physical evidence is even more damning. What more do you need?"

"He still is your son."

"Actually, he's not."

"Whatever are you talking about?"

"Geoffrey is committed to the criminal wing of Harlond State Mental Hospital. I have signed him over as a ward of the state."

"You did what?" Scotch scratched the back of his neck.

"Have you heard from Check?" Lenore put one hand on her hip and the other on the door knob.

"Don't try changing the subject." Scotch prodded. "How could you ...   I can't believe, I don't even want to believe, that you could do such a thing."

Lenore looked up and down the road. Quickly she shifted mental gears. "Geoffrey murdered my husband," Lenore growled. "Do you have any idea of what means?" She jabbed his chest. "Now not only do I want to move forward with my life, but I'd like to give Myles as healthy an upbringing as possible. After a dozen years of having Geoffrey for a brother, that won't be easy. So. if you came here to drag up the past, then please, next time save yourself the trip." She again opened the door and started entering.

Scotch grabbed Lenore's arm. "Look. I'm sorry. Really, I am. These are trying times for us all. I didn't handle that right. I know. But please listen to what I have to say. I still don't think that Geoffrey did it."

Lenore sighed and pulled her face.

"Please, Lenore, hear me out. What if Geoffrey is innocent? That would mean a madman, or woman, could be out there, stalking the entire family. You and Myles may be in grave danger.

A red Ferrari sailed into the driveway.

"Oh shit," she muttered under her breath while bolting past her father.

The ultra-expensive sports car's door opened vertically, like a spaceship hatch.

"So for God's sake, Lenore, pack yours and Myles's bags, and come and stay at the farm." Lenore recoiled.

Wayne Madison alighted his vehicle and strode toward Lenore and Scotch.

"Oh Wayne." Lenore took the gentleman's arm. "You know my father, Scotch Sutton. The lawyer. Remember when he represented the Cricket Club? Well, he's thinking about taking Clark Walden's offer."

Scotch turned to Lenore. His lips silently articulated "What?"

"Scotch Sutton. Of course. Who could ever forget Scotch Sutton." Wayne extended his hand.

A taciturn Scotch allowed Wayne to firmly shake his hand.

"We'll forever be grateful for the big tax break you won us a few years back," Wayne continued. "With class envy the order of the day, the liberal politicians and activists have put their bulls eye target on the Cricket Club's front door. So take Clark's offer and work for us again. Please. We surely need you now more than ever."

"What time are our dinner reservations, Wayne?"

"Eight o'clock."

"Oh my," Lenore looked at her watch, "but we're running late." Lenore grabbed Wayne's arm and pulled him toward the Ferrari. Gingerly she looked back to Scotch. "Call me tomorrow and tell me how your meeting with Clark goes. Good-bye."

Scotch dropped his jaw and scratched his head. Seconds later he put his hands on his hips and clenched his jaw.

Myles, from his bedroom window, spied on his mother riding away in Wayne's Ferrari. He grabbed the same baseball bat that he murdered Yogi with, imagined his pillow as Wayne Madison's head, and started smashing it. Feathers fluttered about his room like snowflakes in a blizzard.

* * *

Secluded in a three-century old Fin de bielle style Philadelphia Society Hill townhouse, the La Cote Lespinasse restaurant earned the distinction of serving the city's finest Parisian cuisine. Inside, pink satin chairs and gilt-framed oil paintings enhanced its milieu of Louis XVI grandeur. Candlelight from 18th century chandeliers cast subdued, shadowy light upon the dapper, formal diners. The cost of a typical three course meal and wine for two at the La Cote Lespinasse often exceeded the price of a travel agency's fully inclusive, three day economy tour of Paris herself.

Lenore and Wayne sat at a Steinway grand piano doubling as a bar. Attired in a natty double breasted, dark blue pinstriped suit, the jockey sized piano player embodied the aura of his song selection. His gravely, septuagenarian singing voice hearkened to a recent, albeit, irretrievably lost Americana. Tempered applause rewarded the coda of his performance. "Thank you." The musician bowed his head. "That selection was of course Johnny Mercer's 'Laura'. Next, I'd like to play for you my favorite Cole Porter song. During the big war, when opening for the Andrew Sisters and Al Jolson on the USO tour, this was my most requested number. I can still do it justice on the ivory, but I'm afraid my old voice is going to need some help with the words. Maybe with some polite urging, Mr. Wayne Madison will accompany me."

Wayne slumped as the eight other piano bar patrons lightly clapped. Finally, a vigorous gentleman wearing a custom Juan Jose Cordova suit pulled Wayne toward the piano bench.

Lenore gasped then straightened her collar on recognizing him- Elizabeth Endicott's older son, Mitchell.

Wayne flushed and held up his hand as he sat beside the piano player. They sang "Night and Day".

Lenore blushed and lowered her head each time Wayne winked or smiled at her as he sang.

Afterward, even the formal diners applauded. The piano player then stood and shook Wayne's hand, seconds later raising it like a victorious boxer's.

"More. We want to hear some more." Mitchell Endicott shouted.

"I'm afraid my old bones need a rest before I can again play for you," the piano player replied. "But Mr. Madison will no doubt continue the entertainment."

The piano bar patrons applauded.

"Thank you." Wayne bowed his head. "After Mr. Charles's performance, I'm better off not attempting any twentieth-century selections. Therefore, I hope you won't mind if I play for you a personal favorite from the Romantic age. Frederic Chopin's Piano Sonata No. 3 in B Minor, op. 58. The Largo. Wayne sat and adroitly played the mesmerizing melody.

After acknowledging the audience's approval, Wayne spoke. "Music can express human feelings and emotions too arcane and deep for words. Often life is a rocky road of pain. Yet we have music to both express and soothe our sorrow. Better is meeting a person who paves that rocky road into a runway. A runway that can launch the human spirit into the sublime realm of the stars. Lenore." Wayne nodded to his date. "I'd like for you to sit next to me while I play for you a special selection."

Lenore felt her heart twirl and rise like sand in a dust devil. She sat deathly still as her view of Wayne blurred.

"Come on. Sit with him," Mitchell Endicott held her arm.

Lenore felt light as a hot-air balloon while floating to Wayne's side.

"Sergei Rachmaninoff's Vocalize, Opus 34, Number 14." Wayne's fingers then did the talking.

During the sublime piece's playing, Lenore saw herself draped in a deep purple velvet, sable fringed gown. She rode a palanquin. Betty Kirby, Hillary Sterling, Dolores Preston, and Helen Murchinson carried each corner. Lenore sniggered at the slaves' agony. Sadistically she laughed as their vertebrae separated like pearls on an over-stretched necklace. "Crack!" Also Lenore's slaves, but overseers, Pat Huggins, Eddie Krause, and Paul Barton whipped their fallen bodies, forcing them to rise and toil some more ... Lenore never heard the piano melody's coda. Wayne broke her reverie by pecking her cheek. He wrapped his arm around her waist and squeezed. The diners heartily applauded.

* * *

"Ha! Ha! Ha! Hey, why aren't you laughing?" Myles turned to the maid. "This a funny show."

Sophie put her hands on hip and bit her lip.

"Ha! Ha! Ha! Did you see that! They just threw a pie in his face! Ha! Ha! Ha!" Myles pointed to the video image of Red Skelton wearing a coconut cream mask.

"I've waited long enough." Sophie lurched over and turned off the T.V. "It's a full hour past your bedtime."

"Hey, turn the T.V. back on!" Myles stood and pointed.

"I'm sorry, but I've played your game long enough. It's time for you to go upstairs and get in bed," the maid prodded.

"My bedtime ain't for another hour." The brat crossed his arms and steeled his mien. "Your mother distinctly told me nine o'clock. It is now ten o'clock. Now go to bed!"

"Oh yeah? My mother says I don't gotta go to bed 'til Red Skelton's over." Myles lurched toward the TV.

Sophie grabbed the brat's arm as he reached for the dial. "You're a lying little boy. Now I've already let you stay up an extra hour. Your mother told you to mind me. So go to bed. Now!"

"Will not!

"Oh yes you will."

"Will not! Will not! Will not! And I don't have to listen to you. You're not my mother! You're just the worker. Ya coon."

"Don't you talk to me like that." Sophie grabbed the brat's shirt sleeve and tugged. "If I have to spank you, I will. Now you 're going upstairs to bed.  Right now!"

"You can't spank me because you're nothin' but an old bag." Myles broke her grip and pulled his face at her.

"You look here," the maid prodded. "You will respect your elders ... Now you're going to bed the hard way." She grabbed the brat's ear lobe.

"Ahh!" Myles screamed as Sophie pulled him through the living room. The instant the maid relaxed her pinch, the brat slipped free and slapped her face.

"Huh!" She gasped and massaged her cheek, owing more to surprise than pain. "Clap!" Sophie returned the favor.

"Ahh!" Myles screamed. In his case, more from pain than surprise. Sizing her up, he realized that close to six decades of hardship and hard work had turned the older woman into a formidable foe. "Ya! Well, I don't wanna watch T.V. anyway!" Myles shouted through his tears. "I wanna play outside." The brat bolted out the front door.

The maid followed. "You get in here this instant." Although the maid commanded a strength and toughness advantage, the twelve-year-old athlete over matched her foot speed by a hare to tortoise margin.

He had already circled to the rear patio and grabbed a football before she caught up to him. "About time you got here. Let's play football. Here you hold for me so I can kick a field goal over that branch."

"You get back inside-- this instant!"

"If you won't hold for me, you can referee." Myles heeled a divot and used it to tee the football. Next the brat kicked the ball over the tree branch. "It's good!" He raised his arms. "Hey raise your damn arms. The kick was good."

"You little devil! Your mother won't let you out of the house for a month, after what I'm going to tell her."

"Shut up!" Myles squared his stance and put hands on hips. "And it's your word against mine. Bitch!"

"That did it! You little monster." Prodding, the maid marched toward the brat.

Myles retreated. Soon he reached his football. The brat picked it up and turned. Sophie was blitzing like Dick Butkis. "Here! Catch!" Myles drilled a spiral into the maid's gut.

"Uhh." She groaned and fell.

The brat put his foot on her and boosted himself toward the kitchen. "Bam!" He slammed the door.

Five minutes later, Sophie rattled the locked door. "Let me in. Please! Let me in. I won't punish you, please, just let me in."

"Ha! Ha! Ha! Ha! Ha! Ha!" Myles sadistically laughed.

After ten minutes, the maid's loud pleading turned to silent sobbing.

The brat snuck and unlocked the door. Sophie stumbled in, "Your cooking also shits." He shoved the pot of goulash off the stove. Stew covered the floor. "Clean it up. Bitch!"

"Young man." After four deep breaths, she prodded and rasped, "You, clean up that mess-- this instant!"

"Fuck you!" He extended his middle finger. "That's your job."

"When your mother gets home . . ."

"When my mother get home, I'll tell 'er you did it. Who do ya think she's gonna believe?" The brat tossed a mop at Sophie's ankles. "Ass-hole!"

Exasperated, the tear, sweat, and dirt-laden maid began mopping.

Myles beamed wider than Betty Kirby did after the late, great Yogi overturned the table at his mother's Eagle Crest Wives tea. Last Spring in shop class, Myles learned how to lathe a block of wood into a bowl. The primary block is never secured to the lathe's spur drive. Rather a secondary block, glued to the primary block with a partitioning piece of paper, is attached to the spur drive. After completing the project, the partitioning paper permits the craftsman to separate the finished bowl without damage. The brat had earlier split the mop shaft and glued it back together in a similar vein. The brat started laughing as Sophie applied more pressure to the mop.

"Snap!" The mop handle broke in two. Sophie fell on her right knee. She gritted her teeth in pain. Eyelids cramped, electric pitchforks flashed across her eyes.

Myles lunged and grabbed the jagged end of the mop handle,

and, with two hands, like Peter Cushing preparing to impale Dracula, cocked it above the maid's prone, writhing body. The brat instead swung the broken shaft downward like a golf club, striking Sophie's injured knee. He flung the stick atop the maid before kicking goulash into her eyes.

* * *

Lenore fawned at Wayne. "Oh Wayne, your playing was just too beautiful. I especially loved the second piece. It was just too special for words."

"Lenore. What an astute observation! You hit the nail right on the head."

Lenore wisely stopped the question '*What do ya mean?*' from reaching her tongue.

Wayne continued. "Rachmaninoff composed and published fourteen songs in 1912 as Opus 34. He based the first thirteen songs on the works of great Russian poets such as Pushkin and Balmont."

"You read Russian poetry?" Lenore's jaw dropped as she craned her face closer to Wayne. "Only the translations. Anyway, the fourteenth song, the one I played, is a vocalize, or wordless song."

"It has such, such, unearthly beauty," Lenore added.

"I couldn't agree more. I find that the song captures the composer's sense of floating melancholia. One can also gain a wonderful sense of floating from the vocalese in Claude Debussy's *Nocturnes*. Wouldn't you agree?

Lenore answered while wiping her lips with a silk serviette: "Yes."

"It seems Lenore, that melancholia is the curse of every creative genius. And you were so right Lenore, Rachmaninoff truly did sublimate his feelings into a melody of unearthly beauty." Wayne smiled approvingly at Lenore. "Unearthly. Great descriptive. As you know Lenore, (She kept her lips covered by the serviette) music aficionados often sight the Neptune movement from Gustav Holst's Planets Suite as a textbook example of a vocalese."

"Yes, um, I'm familiar with that work." Lenore lowered the serviette but pinched her lips between the thumb and forefinger of her other hand.

"Help me Lenore. You seem so adroit with adjectives. Fascinating? Ironic? The most advanced and complex works, the ones mystically transcending human emotions, are associated with astronomical themes. Moreover, they were composed within a decade, plus minus, of the Wright Brother's maiden flight."

"The theme from the movie *2001: A Space Odyssey?* Wasn't

it ...?

"Richard Strauss's symphonic poem: 'Thus Sprach Zarathustra'," Wayne replied. "Good example Lenore. Funny isn't it? Creations of the sober late Romantic mind. I should leave out the late. The C major pedal that launched Strauss's symphony and accompanied the film's opening sunrise, I'm sure you noticed, is similar to the E flat pedal that opens Wagner's Das Rheingold-- composed about a half-century earlier."

Lenore saw a flashback of her late husband discarding a beer bottle labeled, *Rheingold*. "Yes of course. How can anyone not notice?" The recall let her answer with a modicum of sincerity.

"Yet today's hippies have convinced themselves that they need drugs and that clangorous raucous called rock, I won't justify that classification by adding the term, music, to achieve a space-aged, hypnotic effect."

Lenore briefly thought of her brother Check and felt a pang of concern. Smelling Wayne's subtle, expensive aftershave in contrast to Check's not-so-subtle body odor snuffed out the thoughts of her brother. Yet the memory of Lance calling Check her "hippy freak brother" persisted. Wayne was not Lance. Yet. Noting Wayne's impeccable grooming, wherever Check's hideaway ... Lenore shifted to a vision of herself in a wedding dress. She left the church hand in hand with a tuxedoed Wayne Madison. Elizabeth and Fullerton Endicott smiled and showered them with rice ...

"I was just thinking." Wayne broke Lenore's reverie. "With Mitchell in town and Estell on school break, The Endicotts are going to be in Cape May . . ."

A vision attacked her like a pissed-off poltergeist. Stinking of cheap bourbon, a sloshed Pat Huggins stumbled into Wayne, knocking the dashing groom onto his butt. Check, Shaka, Sunman, and Moon child shoved aside the Endicotts. The counter-culture militants snarled and hurled chicken shit on Lenore's wedding gown.

"I'm sorry," Wayne continued. "I was thinking too far ahead. Geoffrey. Yes. I understand he's quite an astronomy enthusiast. Why don't we bring him records of Holst's Planets Suite and Strauss's tone poem, Thus Sprach Zarathustra? I bet he'd appreciate it."

Lenore gasped. She saw her hand wiping chicken-shit from her wedding gown. She looked to the groom for sympathy. Geoffrey replaced Wayne. *I always get you in the end. Ha! Ha! Ha!* The minister, now her father, Scotch Sutton, also laughed at her. *Hey, I got's room for ya in me shack,* offered the best man, filthy, crippled Norman. *Maybe we can talk Horrible Hank into hiring her as a waitress,"* suggested Paul Barton from the front pew. *"Nah."* Eddie Krause shook his head. *"Hank would never go for it. Maybe Madame Misty can hire. . ."*

"I'm sorry Lenore." Wayne clasped her hand. "Seems I struck a raw nerve. If l can ask you to accept my daughter Karen, can't I express compassion for Geoffrey? After all, Lenore, despite what he did, you do want him to get better, don't you?"

"Um, yes, of course," Lenore murmured.

"So, let's bring him those records. After all, Classical music is often used as a form of therapy. Dorothy and I used it to alleviate the symptoms of Karen's autistic disorder."

"Maybe later." A sweat bead emerged on Lenore's forehead. "First I'd just like to ..."

"And who knows?" Wayne interjected. "Maybe Geoffrey didn't do it after all."

"Thank you for saying that, Wayne." Lenore wiped her brow then placed her right hand over Wayne's left hand. "I often find solace in that possibility. I guess we all need faith and hope."

"Here! Here!" Wayne stacked his right hand atop Lenore's left hand and squeezed.

As her left hand started sweating, she pulled it away. Her

head ticced in four different directions. She noticed Wayne had shrugged and slanted his head. *'Think fast.'* Lenore then spoke, "Everything here is so overwhelming. Your music, this restaurant's decor and atmosphere, and the menu," she next pointed to an open menu. "Just reading it ... It's exquisite. Chateaubriand. Veal Medaillons in Madeira sauce. Stuffed quail with pheasant and a wild mushroom salad. But they list no prices."

"Ahh ..." Wayne held up his hand. "Would such an elegant establishment ever be so uncouth as to stoop to the vulgarity of money?"

"Then how do you...?

"Shh...Wayne placed forefinger before bunched lips. "They discretely send its members a bill at the end of the month. In a plain brown envelope." Wayne looked at Lenore with a straight face. Seconds later he laughed.

Lenore also chuckled. "O.K. you got me there. So, what are you having? It's all so exquisite.

I could never decide."

"I was thinking the Frog legs in a truffle sauce. I know it sounds exotic, but it tastes just like good old American country fried chicken ..."

Lenore's mind flashed back to her childhood. Although the

twelve-year-old lawyer's daughter attended the Bohm School for girls, she also had household chores. Each morning Scotch assigned his daughter the task of cleaning the chicken cages ... Chicken shit ... Angrily, sullenly, albeit silently, Lenore scrunched her nose as she swept stinking chicken droppings, looking to her like so many gobs of puss encasing green yolks of phlegm, from cage bottom to pale. She did manage to tolerated her duties as a farmgirl. Yet, *'Shut up! Shut up!'* She covered her ears and screamed as Betty Norton led her more affluent school mates in the taunt: "Manicure, hairdo, Lenore stinks of chicken-do."

"Lenore! What's wrong? You suddenly look sick."

"Um, I'm sorry Wayne. I guess it's the thought of eating a reptile that lived in a swamp."

"Okay then, how about we dine on something from the sea?" Wayne covered his face with the menu. "How does the Lobster Terrine sound to you? Dorothy relished it. I had an impossible time convincing her to order anything else."

Lenore gasped. Regaining her composure, she asked: "Just lobster?"

"Ahh ... As Dorothy always said, 'more than just lobster'."

Lenore nibbled her fingernails. A memory haunted her. The Minute Man Insurance picnic. Lance chomped on a burnt hot dog and said to his favorite cronies. "Well, it's a damn sight better than my wife's cooking." Pat Huggins, Eddie Krause, and Paul Barton looked in her direction and laughed.

Wayne placed his menu on the table, returning Lenore to the present. "Try shellfish with green beans, tomato, and shredded carrots; all topped with celery remoulade." He pointed upward. "An impeccable mustard sauce. It's our chef, Jean Jacques De Luz's, specialty."

"Jean Jacques De Luz ...     That name ... Wasn't he Charles DeGaulle's personal favorite?

How on Earth did a Philadelphia restaurant ever get ...?"

"Shh." Wayne again placed forefinger before bunched lips. "What was that vulgar thing that one never mentions at the La Cote Lespinasse?"

Lenore chuckled. "Touche. You got me again."

"If you think the menu's overwhelming, wait until you see the wine list." Wayne leaned closer and turned a page of her menu.

Lenore gasped. She didn't recognize a single selection. Instead, she pictured Lance adding Schmidt's beer to her shopping list.

"Forgive me for unoriginality ..." Wayne looked at the wine

list.

Lenore, realizing that Wayne failed to notice her unease, sighed in relief and grinned. "But," he continued, "I think I'll stay with my old friend, Dom Perignon."

"No. Not unoriginal," Lenore added. "Wise. I can't think of a more perfect combination.

Lobster Terrine and Dom Perignon." She beamed.

* * *

Tony Bennett's 'I *Left My Heart in San Francisco,* played on the radio as Wayne downshifted his Ferrari into the Burkett's driveway. Wayne reached for his door handle; Lenore leaned over and clutched his arm. "Rather you don't walk me to the front door. I don't think Myles is used to my dating yet."

"I only glanced at him, but he did seem a bit piqued."

"Don't worry about him." Lenore dropped her hand to Wayne's thigh. "I'm sure he'll come around. After all, I doubt very much that he'll consider his mother dating the end of the world. I think that soon he'll like the idea of again having a man in his life."

"Maybe I should come to his next football game."

"Yes. That might not be a bad idea." Lenore leaned closer. "Shh ..." Lenore put her finger before bunched lips. "We have plenty more time to discuss our kids." Shifting her hand to his waist, her elbow accidentally hit the radio's tuning dial. The drum solo from Iron Butterfly's *'In-A-God-Da-Da-Vida'* played. "Rather we snuggle right here in your car." Lenore's heart thumped harder than the drum beat.

Wayne never thought to change the station. He passionately kissed Lenore.

* * *

"What on Earth happened here?" Lenore dropped her jaw at the sight of the disheveled maid and ransacked the house. "Your son. Your son." Sophie prodded with jittery finger.

"Mommy! Mommy!" Myles ran down the stairs and hugged Lenore. "She beat me!" He bawled.

"Is that true?" Lenore glowered at the maid. "Yes but . . ."

"Waaaaa!" Myles wailed.

"So, you beat my son," Lenore snarled. "I didn't hire you to..."

"But, but . . ."

"No buts," Lenore prodded at the maid.

"Mommy. She spilled the pot of stew. Then she made me clean it. When I didn't do it fast enough for her, she started hittin' me with a mop handle. She hit me so hard that it broke! Look I'll show you." Myles ran into the kitchen and emerged with the broken mop. "See what she did!" Myles lowered his pajama bottoms to reveal a deep, red, self-inflicted welt.

"You ... You ... Monster!" Lenore lurched forward and slapped Sophie's face harder than ever she struck her late husband.

Sophie massaged her cheek, wincing in pain. "You don't understand, Mrs. Burkett, listen to me. Please!"

"Listen to you? I've seen all I need to hear. Now get out!" Lenore prodded. "Get out right now or I'll call the police. And, oh, after I'm finished talking to the agency ... After they hear what I have to say about you, you will never, ever, work again."

Sophie murmured in a Slavic tongue.

"I said, Get out! Now!" Lenore flared her arms. The maid glanced at Myles pulling his cheeks apart and sticking out his tongue as she left. Lenore slammed the door behind her.

"Mommy!" Myles hugged Lenore and squalled. "Please don't hire another maid. We don't need anyone else. I can do everything for you. Give me a chance to show you. Please."

"We'll see, honey." Lenore patted Myles's back. "We'll see."

# Chapter 7

Dr. Tryvye nibbled on his lower lip and slanted his head as the steel ball turned west. Labyrinth trap 46. Northward past 49, North-east between 50 and 51-- just eight more to go! The psychiatrist nearly whiplashed himself as two stout fingers pinched the ball from the playing surface.

Scotch Sutton smirked as he tossed the ball upward and caught it.

After surveying his toy's empty gaming field, the doctor cleared his throat and looked toward the grandfather. "Hmm...Ahh, I don't believe that you are among my patients. See my receptionist in the waiting room. I'm sure she can fit you in with an appointment."

"I'm not a prospective patient. I came to talk about a patient. Geoffrey Burkett."

"Geoffrey Burkett. Hmm Ahh, yes, fascinating case." Dr. Tryvye pointed to the ceiling. "Fascinating. Patricide. You understand, sir, that Geoffrey Burkett's actions are a manifestation of how primitive man once symbolized their groups with a totem. This totem was often an animal. Early society cast taboos against killing, eating, or even touching it. On special occasions, however, the savages would ritually slaughter and eat their totem animal. Thus the totem meal. Perhaps man's earliest festival. A single, powerful male dominated ancient man's small hordes. This male not only kept all the females for himself, but he also expelled his younger male rivals, thus preventing incest and encouraging the formation of sexual ties outside the cohort. You see! You see!" The psychiatrist flapped his hands. "Although civilized man has abjured such atavistic rites, the manifestations of this early ceremony still linger in the contemporary subconscious. Modem man often apportions his father as this dominant male. Sometimes the father is even cast in the role of the totem animal. A totem often symbolizes the oppressive moral restrictions of not only social organization and religion but also the super-ego. Occasionally a disturbed person's Id will further cognify the father's exclusive retaining of the mother, as a synonymous extension of the dominant male of the primal clan's exploitative avidity. You see! You see!" The psychiatrist repeatedly jutted his head parrot-like. "This compels the unbalanced Id son to vicariously reenactment the atavistic ritual of the totem meal by slaying his father." Dr. Tryvye grinned and folded his hands behind his head.

Scotch pulled his face and shook his head.

"Aren't you a little late?" Dr. Tryvye skewed his head. "That I've already explained at the press conference. Now if you will excuse me, I've got more important ..."

"Plonk!" Scotch tossed the steel ball onto the labyrinth. Dr. Tryvye flinched.

"I'm not a reporter. My name is Scotch Sutton. The boy's grandfather." Scotch braced his arms on the doctor's aircraft carrier sized desk and leaned forward. "If I want to hear about totems and taboos, I'll watch Chief Halftown on T.V. You've got my grandson confined in Harlond State's ward for the criminally insane..."

"Technically, sir, he is no longer your grandson."

"Officially, sir, I am his attorney." Scotch dropped his business card before the psychiatrist. "Hmm ... Ahh." Dr. Tryvye perused the card. "Need I remind you, the insane have no rights."

"As individuals, you are correct. As a group, however, legal reforms are now in place. I'll spare you the legal jargon, but, in a nutshell, you are illegally confining Geoffrey Burkett. State mental institutions can only confine patients who were convicted, then acquitted by reason of insanity, to their criminal ward. Geoffrey Burkett was never convicted, nor did he ever confess to a crime. Moreover, he is a minor. *Manifestly,* a violation. Hmm ... Ahh?" Scotch pointed to the ceiling.

"Hmm. . . Ahh, yes, what you must understand, however, is that the boy is suffering a classic manifestation of the self-imposed anxiety manifesting from denial. Harland State is a place of treatment, not punishment. Providing a positive stimulus, the desire for a better living environment may help the boy to cognify the reality of his heinous misdeed."

"I see Comrade Stalin. The truth is but a political construct. The ends justify the means. What we must achieve from the detainee is the desired outcome. A confession."

"I assure you, sir, that the psychiatric community is acting in the best interests of the patient. He manifestly suffers from an antisocial personality disorder, or APO for short."

"An APO huh." Scotch scratched his brow. "Is one of those a psychotic sociopath?"

"No.   But that's the purpose of his treatment at Harland State. To prevent that final declension."

"So. you are going to accomplish that by locking the boy up with madmen?"

"Madmen? Colloquial contumelies. Nevertheless, Geoffrey, to a manifestly pathological degree, has fallen prey to the universal obsessional neurosis of religion."

"Forgive my sarcasm of a moment ago, but may I once again cite the Soviet Union. Do they not lock up their God believers in insane asylums?"

"Yes, but . . ."

"What does the fact that the Berlin wall is about five times higher than the wall surrounding Harland State tell you?"

Dr. Tryvye shrugged his shoulders.

"It tells me," Scotch continued, "that their entire system is insane. Especially the belief that religious people are crazy. Like Henry David Thoreau wrote, the inmates may be the sane. I make my point by analogy. In the matter of my grandson, it seems that the doctors are the…"

"Red-baiting. Utterly irrelevant to the Geoffrey Burkett case. Need I remind you, Mr. Sutton, many believe that America is a mistake. A giant mistake. Geoffrey has chosen religious beliefs as a protection against the danger of certain neurotic afflictions. By accepting this universal neurosis, he attempts to spare himself the task of forming a personal neurosis. Moreover, the boy has fabricated his own apostle, so to speak. He attributes his escapist verbiage to a fantasized wise man named Norman. Positively the manifestation of a disturbed, unhinged mind. So please, Mr. Sutton, don't interfere. The psychiatric community knows what's best for Geoffery Burkett."

"An imaginary apostle named Norman, huh?" Scotch scratched his head. "My apologies Dr. Tryvye. You are correct. The psychiatric community does know what's best for Geoffrey. I'll leave my grandson in your capable hands." Scotch turned and headed for the door.

Dr. Tryvye grinned and returned the steel ball to the Labyrinth playing field.

He tensed his lips as the ball rolled past trap 52 ...

"But perhaps the legal community knows what's best for the psychiatric community." *Plunk.* The steel ball fell into trap 53. "What the . . .?"

Scotch Sutton approached the doctor's desk. "Elizabeth Endicott has arranged a personal audience with the Governor of Pennsylvania for me tomorrow, noon. We have already established that your confining thirteen-year-old Geoffrey Burkett to Harland State's criminal ward is a manifest violation of two state laws. Tomorrow I will initiate legal proceedings to the effect. The Governor will, of course, suspend all funding to the hospital pending investigation. The Psychiatric board won't be too happy about that, will they? After the investigation ascertains Harlond State's guilt, the Attorney General will levy a heavy fine. Since you will be identified as the perpetrator, I think you know what will happen to your professional standing. You will be as welcome at Harlond State as an Army recruiter at Woodstock. Even if you do keep your license, after the scandal-mongering press besmirches your reputation, you will have as many patients in private practice as the Apollo 11 astronauts found on the moon. Hmm," Scotch pinched his chin, "Ahh," he pointed to the ceiling.

"Hmm," Dr. Tryvye rubbed his goatee, "Ahh ...Yes!" He beamed and shook his fist.

"I have achieved a breakthrough analytic realization! I have discussed with Geoffrey, rewarding his cooperation with a private room. With carpets, a real bed, a desk, and a window with a view. Granting him such an award may give him the positive stimulus to more liberally share his free associations. A more tranquil, hospitable environment can only assuage his inner conflicts and help him codify the reality of his actions. Yes. Yes. Yes. I will move him first thing tomorrow."

"Today." Scotch braced his arms on the psychiatrist's desk.

"Today?" Dr. Tryvye scratched his brow. "Even better!"

"And that includes visitation rights."

"Hmm ... Ahh. Contact with the outside world. Again I have achieved a key analytic realization. Reality can only enhance the patient's recovery. I will schedule you a propitious visit. Thank you for your cooperation." The psychiatrist started playing with his Newton's Cradle. The clacking cloaked the sound of Scotch Sutton closing the door.

# Chapter 8

"... And the embroidered Porthault table cloths," Betty Kirby clutched Hillary Sterling's wrist. "Giving a traditional Thanksgiving banquet a continental touch ..."

Lenore sat at a corner table. She snipped yet another turkey from construction paper and pasted on yet another honeycomb, fan like crape paper tail. "But Hillary ..."

"... What a divine idea," Betty continued. "How impressed the invitees will be with your first function as committee vice-president."

"Hillary, I ..." Lenore shrank as her voice crumbled.

"Well admittedly I took a chance with the Porthault tablecloths," Hillary smacked her lips. "But every rousing success derives from risk. I just hope Elizabeth's little gamble pays like mine. After all, Billy White Eagle. Yes. Without doubt, he's a renowned chef ... But can you depend on him to show up sober? You know how they are."

"Hillary!" Lenore, feeling as a child just told to wait an extra two weeks for Christmas, clipped the construction paper like a chain gang convict slashing weeds.

"Even if he doesn't," Betty braced her arm on Hillary's

shoulder, "after they eat his brandied apples ... It won't matter! So either way, the guests will rate your banquet as the best ever! Te he he."

Hillary also giggled.

"Hillary!" Lenore stood. "I suggest ..."

"The event that I most anticipate," Hillary clutched Betty's arm and walked her away from Lenore's table, "is the Endicott's New Year's Eve party. That's when I plan on making the connection between Estelle and my Cornelius."

"Hillary!" Lenore walked toward the vice chairwoman and Betty. "I suggest that we ..."

Betty prodded. "I suggest that you cut out those turkeys a little more carefully. They're starting to look like ... Chickens!  Te he he!"

"Hillary!" Lenore growled and prodded at Betty. "Elizabeth Endicott dismissed her from your sub-committee. She assigned me in her place. Now I think that we should ..."

"I think that what infected Janet Boyer got to Elizabeth Endicott." Betty stepped toward Lenore. "Putting you on the committee? At first, I thought she was just trying to be funny. After all, the Windsor members not regarding you with contempt, look upon you with amusement. Only Janet Boyer granted you a modicum of respect and look at what happened to her. Look at what happened to your son! After Elizabeth joins them, Hillary will run the show. Then maybe, just maybe, Windsor will let you in the back door . . . As a uniformed maid!"

Lenore's face twisted like a malefic beast's. She unsheathed her finger nails ... A gentle hand unexpectedly soothed her waist. Lenore started, then just as quickly smiled. Wayne Madison.

"Exciting news honey. Liz here has invited us for a New York evening. We'll travel with her husband and Marion in their private railroad coach. From the station, it's by limousine to the Metropolitan Opera and *Lohengrin* from their exclusive box."

Elizabeth Endicott smiled and nodded.

Betty Kirby's bladder tingled as it did back in the second grade when, thinking her teacher was out of the classroom, she referred to her as 'The fat old bitch'. Discovering Miss McGillicuddy in the corner of the room, eight-year-old Betty lost it. Fortunately, only an embarrassing puddle rather than the more severe consequence of her teacher hearing the epithet. Thirty-five-year-old Betty blanched as a long-dead memory vivified like a zombie from *'The Night of the Living Dead.'* Her father felt guilty after another Cognac bender at the Cricket Club's teak bar. Driving home, Burleigh Norton purchased a baby blue clad, fabric dolly from a vendor at a stop light. He arrived home and dropped it at his ten-year-old daughter's feet. Foggily he staggered toward the bathroom. "You drunk fuck," little Betty whispered to herself the recently learned, all-purpose all-purpose profanity.

"A girl dolly wears pink."

He heard her! Turning like a gunfighter, the father stamped forward, snatched the dolly, then tore it's damn arm off! He raked Betty's hair and jammed the severed limb, stuffing first, into his little girl's mouth.

The musty, gritty-tasting thing sponged her mouth dry. Nothing left for tears. His hand thunder clapped her cheek. Bells clashed with, "You spoilt, dirty rotten little wench." *Why did Daddy call me a hardware tool,'* she wondered while falling to her side.

Betty, years later, forgave her father only because changing times unearthed stories of daddies sticking far worse things in their little girl's mouths. Nevertheless, the incident created an aversion that forever haunted her marital relations. Is that what drove Johnny to Madame Misty? Ardently Betty squeezed her urethra as considering the ramifications of Elizabeth Endicott overhearing her tirade superseded all thought.

"What do you think?" Wayne asked

"Wonderful! Too good to be true." Lenore answered. "Even

if I don't know a word of Italian."

Elizabeth Laughed.

"My lady's got a great sense of humor, doesn't she Liz?"

"You can say that." Elizabeth replied as she walked away with Wayne and Lenore.

A parched Betty remained ashen long after the three left the Cricket Club dining room. Even Hillary mocking Lenore as a common, vulgar, uncultured, uncultivated, ignorant peon clod for thinking that *Lohengrin* was sung in Italian failed to revive her.

# Chapter 9

From a hilltop prospectus one could look over Harland State Mental Hospital's parameter wall and picture the 480-acre compound as a Medieval fortress. The main structure sat on a glacis. Its imposing scale, stone construction, crenelated roof facade, and three-story high Lancet windows at its flanks inspired Gothic imaginings. Otherwise, its unadorned veneer, grayish color, flat slab-roof, and boxy shape spelled I-n-s-t-i-t-u-t-i-o-n. A cold, bare-treed, dishwater gray late November day such as this, did, however, inspire visions of castle dungeons. Unfortunately for Geoff Burkett, he lived in such a hell hole.

By now, Geoffrey had divided his life into before and after his imprisonment. His life before consisted of mere flashes of memory. Sometimes he heard the condemnations of his mother, the taunts of his brother, and even specters of his angry late father. Visions of his beloved, deceased Yogi dog and Lee Lee cat kindled tears of grief. Tears, even if burning like acid, nevertheless, confirmed for Geoffrey his fleeting humanity. Moreover, intense prayer instilled hope for an actual eternity above and beyond his seeming eon here below-- prayers that blocked this echo chamber's amplification of incessant pacing footsteps, mad ravings, and masturbatory moans.

Knees on the white porcelain floor, Geoff rested his elbows on his metal cot. Often when praying he would glance upward and picture the high, flat porcelain ceiling as a dome adorned with Michelangelo and Titian imagery. At this moment he looked up and imagined the ceiling parting like Moses's Red Sea. A Technicolor rainbow arched across a vast, purple-clouded sky ...

"He don't listen to father killers, ya little mother-fucker!" the madman in the adjacent cell yelled. "Only the King of the Underworld rules in this subterranean abode!" The unclothed madman stuck his member between the cell bars and flagellated. "One fine day, they'll let me shower with you, father killer! Here's what's waiting for you!" The madman masturbated.

"No! No!" Geoff covered his eyes. "Shut up! Shut up!"

"HA! HA! HA! HA! HA! HA! My little gift from Satan!"

Geoffrey buried his eyes into his thin straw mattress, covered his ears, and screamed.

Dr. Tryvye and a senior guard entered the ward. The psychiatrist pointed to the raving lunatic dubbed *Rabies.'* Like Marlon Perkins sedating a beast on Geoffrey's favorite TV show, *The Wild Kingdom,* the senior guard shot the madman with a tranquilizing dart.

"Ahh!" Rabies yelled. He hopped about his cell like a mad

ape. Seconds later he fainted and slept on the floor.

Dr. Tryvye and the senior guard then advanced on Geoffrey's cell. The young boy now screamed with inflamed vigor.

"Ah, ah, ah, no need for that." Dr. Tryvye prodded. "This time I'm the bearer of good tidings. Remember that room I told you about? The one with a real bed, bathroom, carpet, and a window? Well as a reward for your cooperation, I've decided to move you upstairs."

Geoff tapered his screams to steady gasps.

"Not that I think you need this, but it is procedure." Dr. Tryvye nodded to the senior guard. Five minutes later, they were escorting a straitjacketed, sobbing Geoffrey to his new quarters.

# Chapter 10

The Stanforth community dealt with the Lance Burkett murder as humans are wont in the aftermath of wars, natural disasters, or governments of inhumane insanity. They stashed it in their mind's attic and forgot. The line was now clear. Her dream romance with the Main Line's most eligible widower advanced as if pulled by a GG I locomotive. Myles's resistance to Wayne, nonetheless, waved the caution flag. Yet Wayne invited them both for a weekend at his Cape May Beach mansion, thus switching her romance back to the fast track. The New York evening with Wayne and the Endicotts surpassed Lenore's wildest schoolgirl fantasy. Only Wayne saying that Dorothy preferred Verdi and Puccini to Wagner bothered her. Otherwise, the occasion awed her to the point of not figuring that Lohengrin was sung in German until Elsa's Einsam in Truben Tagen nearly midway through Act I.

Elizabeth Endicott orchestrated the Cricket Club's Thanksgiving banquet in three courses as successfully as the Metropolitan Opera did Richard Wagner's romantic music drama in three acts. Billy White Eagle's roast goose, wild rice, and brandied apples tasted delicious by any gourmet's standard. Yet for Lenore the cuisine and occasion lagged well behind the elation of joining Wayne Madison at the Endicott's table. Even better was the delicacy of watching Betty Kirby and Hillary Sterling stew at their tables of lesser caste.

For Betty Kirby, jealousy over Lenore's sudden rise in status placed a distant second to fear.

Each paranoiac glance at Elizabeth Endicott seemed to produce a different look of scorn. *'Did she hear me? Maybe she didn't. What if she did? I don't think so. But she was standing so close. How close? When did she walk in? Wayne and Elizabeth entered so quietly, so unexpectedly. For how long was she standing there? Maybe she heard but didn't care. How could she not care? Did she already forget. What if she never forgets?'* Betty's stomach churned like a lawn mower. She couldn't even enjoy Hillary Sterling challenging Wayne Madison's sanity for his romantic interest in Lenore Burkett.

They had forgotten Lance Burkett. Fortunately, one remembered Geoff Burkett.

The distance not hobbled was hitchhiked. A lift in the back of a pick-up truck covered much of the distance. During a ride with beer reveling teenagers, Norman, unfortunately, after disclosing his destination, got ejected. After two hours of sweat, abrasion, and road grime, he stumbled into the Yorkshire Township Police Station.

"Well, if it isn't crazy old Norman Bell." Nineteen-year-old patrolman D.R. Abiger approached the walnut swing gate. His oblique face hinted country inbreeding. The crew cut rookie cop's jutting ears looked like open taxi-cab doors. "Getting cold outside, huh? So, you're here to check into our poky for the winter? Well, I suggest you hop a Florida-bound freight. 'Cause there ain't no room at this here inn."

"Let me tell you something boy. I've been in this town since steam pulled the Paoli Local, and I ain't never once spent a second in Stanforth's little house."

"Who's calling who boy? Boy. You who look like some good old boys stuffed ya down a smokestack."

"You better show some respect for your elders." Norman pointed his cane at the punk. "I've struggled all my life just keepin' alive. Seein' that you're still livin' with your mama, that's still sumptin ya got to learn. Now I came to talk to the man."

"Shining shoes." D.R. Abiger smirked. "I guess you're too dumb to know that you now need a permit to shine shoes on my sidewalks. Hell. If not for the Endicotts, you'd've been run out of here long ago."

"Hey. Hey. Enough of this!" Police Chief O'Shaughnessy stepped between the old man and young boy. ''Patrolman Abiger." Michael O'Shaughnessy looked at his watch. "It's time you relieve

McMichaels and direct traffic on Lancaster Avenue. Okay, Mr. Bell. You've got two minutes. State your business."

"I've got two minutes? State my business? Not you too. Are you forgetting the time you climbed down a manhole as a seven-year-old boy? Who heard you cryin' like a baby and pulled you out?"

Noticing his female receptionist trying to stifle laughter, Chief O'Shaughnessy held up his hand. "All right. All right. I'm sorry." The police chief then put his hand on Norman's back and led him into his office. "Have a seat." He closed the door.

Norman sat.

"Okay. What is it you want?

"It's Geoffrey Burkett. You've got an innocent young boy locked up for somethin' he didn't do." Chief O'Shaughnessy sighed. "I do have an innocent person locked-up, do I? Normally one advances to detective from patrolman, not from shoe shiner. I'm sorry. I didn't mean for it to come out that way. Look. The evidence is overwhelming and conclusive. We found his belongings all over the crime sight. The murder weapon, covered with his fingerprints, was found on the boy. Moreover, the victim's blood was all over the boy's clothing."

"Someone could have planted it on him." Norman raised his

hands

"Alright." Chief O'Shaughnessy hardened his mien. "Motive. We have established that Geoffrey Burkett was physically abused by his father. Recently this has caused the boy to erupt in violence. Just last month he beat a schoolmate to the point of hospitalization. That got him suspended."

"Bart Hatcher? You got no idea how long and hard that bully provoked Geoffrey."

"I have no idea," the police chief said wryly. "Provoked. My point exactly. Geoffrey Burkett snapped after watching his father kill his pet cat."

"Lance Burkett didn't kill Geoff's cat. I got her livin' with me now."

"You've got everybody's cat living with you. Look, Norman. I've got the testimony of two reliable eyewitnesses. Geoffrey attacked his father for killing his cat. The only logical conclusion, from every conceivable piece of evidence, is, that Geoffrey regrouped his thoughts and killed his father in cold blood. Yes. My patrolman did speak out of line. But he does make a point. Vagrancy and shining shoes without a license, which we would never grant, are illegal in Yorkshire township. Only because of the Endicott's charity have we shown you such tolerance. Think of this township as a boat. Think of me as the captain. Think of yourself as a stowaway." Chief O'Shaughnessy prodded. "So, I don't suggest rocking my boat."

"Your boat?" Norman leaned on his cane. "Well, your boat has a leak. I suggest you repair that leak, instead of tryin' to stop your boat from sinkin' by throwin' an innocent passenger to the sharks. Now you got the hungriest shark of 'em all swimin' *in* your boat. If you don't catch him, he's gonna eat a whole lot more of your passengers."

"Patrolman Abiger." Chief O'Shaughnessy stood. "Give Norman a ride back to the train station. Here. Take some of these with you." The police chief pushed a plate of doughnuts toward Norman and walked away.

Norman stuffed two doughnuts into his coat pockets. "Sharks eat a lot more than doughnuts. A whole lot more."

Chief O'Shaughnessy ignored the old man.

# Chapter 11

Lenore regressed from strumming her fingers on her dining room tabletop to scratching it. Four o'clock, Friday afternoon. Late autumn's early darkness was worming in like a Nordic fog. Wayne was a half hour late for their much anticipated Cape May weekend. Even worse, she had no clue as to Myles's whereabouts. '*Where the hell is he?*' Lenore thought. Merely considering Myles torpedoing her grand opportunity put her on the brink of anxiety's next step down. Chewing the carpet. She did see a bright side to Wayne's tardiness. At least she had a chance to secure Myles before Wayne's arrival.

"How-word is a cow-word. He never takes a show-word. He smells like the S-word"

Myles's voice. Lenore's spirits rode the penthouse express elevator, even if he was playing with the junior member of York Place's Lumpen clan.

She sprung out the back door. To her chagrin, she discovered that Myles, clad in mud-caked, tattered trousers and a gritty sweatshirt, looked more derelict than Howard Hildebrandt.

"Here! Catch this Cow-weird!" Myles drilled a football into Howard's hands. He dropped it. "Hey! Play fair." Howard shook the sting out of his fingers.

"Myles!" Lenore marched toward her son. "Get in here. Now! Wayne will be here any minute."

"I don't wanna go to the shore with Wayne. I wanna stay here and play football. How-weird! Throw me the ball!"

The Hildebrandt boy tossed Myles the football.

"Hey Mom. You can play with us. Let's play keep-away. You're it!" Myles pointed at Lenore.

"You get inside and clean up." Lenore, prodding, advanced on Myles.

"Keep away." The brat tossed the ball over his mother's head then sidestepped her blitz. Lenore stumbled past.

"Throw me the ball, How-weird!"

"You give me that!" Lenore charged Howard.

The Hildebrant boy, confused, inadvertently lofted the ball over Lenore's head. Myles caught it. "Good one Howeird. Keep away from mom!"

"Dammit. Get inside!" Tears punctuated her shrieks as she pivoted back to Myles.

"Only if you can catch me" Myles ran serpentine.

Lenore chased him like a vertigo victim.

"Here, Howeed." Running past, Myles shuffled the ball to the Hildebrandt boy. "Throw me a pass! Mom's the defender!"

Lenore Burkett reminded no one of Lance Burkett as she tried to flag her disobedient son. A perplexed Howard threw the ball errantly.

Wayne's Ferrari had stalked into the driveway silently as a Leopard shadowing its quarry. He scooped up the ball on the second bounce. "Go out for a pass Myles." Wayne cocked his arm. "Howard can defend."

Myles clenched his fists and flared his arms. "No way man! My father was a college All-American quarterback." The brat prodded. "You ain't even my father!"

"I'll make you a deal. Go out for a pass. If I don't throw you a perfect touchdown spiral, you don't have to go to the shore. If I do, you do as your mother tells you." Myles scratched his forehead.

"Well," Wayne continued. "Show me you're as good as your mother tells me you are. Go out for a pass. Howard. You defend. If you can intercept, I'll drive you to and from school in my Ferrari every day next week."

"Cool! You're on. Come on Myles." Howard bumped into the brat.

Myles reluctantly trotted away. Four steps later he shifted into his best sprinter's gate. Wayne spiraled the football on a low arc.

Howard turned and leapt for it. He extended his fingers. The breeze tingled his fingertips as the ball flew millimeters above.

"Thud." The football stuck in Myles's hands. He wanted oh so badly to drop it. That synapse failed to click. Myles held it like a precious, antique China bowl filled with excrement.

"You made a deal honey," Lenore walked over to Wayne.

"Ya. I heard you myself," Howard added.

"Shut up. Everybody shut up!" The brat screamed.

* * *

Mile's rode in the Ferrari's rear jump seat. He leaned between Wayne and Lenore's front bucket seats and pointed at the speedometer. "Hey, does this car really go a hundred and eighty miles-per-hour?"

"She sure does," Wayne answered. "Bull! I don't believe you."

"You don't? Well, I just raced her in the Italian Grand Prix. I'll happily show you my timeslip."

"Bet you didn't win."

"Racing in the Italian Grand Prix isn't about winning or losing. It's about the thrill of competing."

"Ya?" the brat retorted. ''My football coach says winning isn't everything: it's the only thing."

"Well, just finishing is a moral victory."

"My coach also says moral victories are for losers. So what does that make you?" The brat guffawed.

"Myles!" Lenore interjected. "That wasn't a very nice thing to say. Apologize right now."

"Will not! And he's a liar too. This thing don't go no 180 Miles-per-hour. How can it? After all, the Italians put screen doors on their submarines. Ha! Ha! Ha!"

"Tell you what Myles, I can't drive very fast here in this Schuylkill Expressway traffic, but when we hit the Atlantic City Expressway, I'll take 'er up to a hundred. Have you ever ridden that fast before?"

"Who cares how fast you can drive this spaghetti mobile? Bet you can't run faster than a nigger."

"Myles!" Lenore turned and scowled at her brat. "That's enough! No more bad language."

"Ya? Well let's see *him* do something about it."

"Myles. I may not be your father, but I am your elder. I don't care about what you say to me, but if you don't start respecting your mother, you're going to find yourself in some very unexpected trouble. Understand?"

The firmness of Wayne's voice shattered the brat's bravado. Myles slumped and sulked. Twenty minutes later, the Ferrari crossed the Delaware River via the Walt Whitman Bridge, entering New Jersey. Lenore placed her hand on Wayne's shoulder and leaned toward him.

"Hey!" Myles wedged his arms between them. "Don't sit so close!"

During the 45-minute drive across southern New Jersey, the brat, sandwiching his chaperoning head between Wayne and his mother, enforced a stony silence.

"See the bay, Myles?" Wayne, at last, broke the discomfiting hush. "We're almost there."

"Ya. I see the bay," the brat replied. "Of course, I smelled it ten minutes ago. Your house doesn't stink like dead fish too, does it?"

Wayne sighed and shook his head.

Lenore tightened her lips.

* * *

The extreme southeast edge of the state of New Jersey ends in a fifteen-mile-long by eight-mile-wide peninsula. That tongue of land divides the Atlantic Ocean and Delaware Bay. Cape May sits at its point. Ferrari headlights cast ghostly reflections upon the fashionable summer community's closed bakeries, gift shops, and ice cream parlors. Yet in Cape May one can discover historic, beachfront Victorian mansions. Wayne Madison stopped at such a home. Flanked by the Endicott and Garvos properties, Wayne's twenty-room house featured wide viewing balconies and domed pavilion rooms.

"Is this place yours?" Myles pointed at Wayne's mansion.

"Sure is." Wayne placed his foot on his Ferrari's bumper and rested his forearm over his knee. "Your home for the weekend."

''No way Jose." Myles brushed his hands at the house. "I'm not sleeping in that place. It's haunted man."

"Oh, only by Casper and his friendly buddies. Maybe if you're lucky, they'll appear and talk some football with you."

"Huh." Myles shrugged and pulled his face. "Sure. If they do, I bet they'll know a lot more about it than you do."

"Myles!" Lenore shouted.

Wayne held his hand up toward Lenore and looked at Myles. "Well, if they don't, seeing that it's almost winter, we'll have the entire beach to ourselves to play some football."

The brat pulled his face.

Wayne then popped his car's trunk and heaved Lenore's suitcase.

Suddenly Myles snatched it with a thief s guile. "Da-da-da, da; eek, eek." Carrying his mother's bag to the house's threshold, he vocalized the theme from the T.V. show, *The Adams Family.*

Within the hour Wayne had flames roaring in the stone fireplace. He offered to order a pizza, with the works, big as his Ferrari' s wheels. Myles responded by telling a stale Italian joke. "The only thing a real man eats is a thick, juicy steak," he added.

Wayne left for the kitchen's walk in cooler. Presto! He returned with an inch-thick Texas T-bone. It sizzled as he grilled it in the fireplace alongside an Idaho potato. The aroma of barbecue char steeped the room

Myles devoured the manly meal with lion rapacity. Only after his mother's prodding did the brat grunt "thank you" to the gentleman.

After a creme de menthe parfait desert, Wayne lyrically described a sunrise over the ocean. Myles assured that *he* would share it with his mother by creeping into her bed a half-hour after lights out.

* * *

The unseasonably warm December morning felt more as an October afternoon. Wayne's seal fur Amundsen coat, secured by polished beluga teeth, and Lenore's goose down, Aspen ski jacket, moreover, warmed them like an August sun. A midst chirping, swooping seagulls, Wayne and Lenore strolled hand in hand on fluffy sands. Each roaring breaker freshened the air with a salty scent.

Lenore turned to the gentleman, taking both of his hands. "My, but do I hope you appreciated growing up with all of this."

"Yes. My family has owned this estate since the first World War." Wayne wryly smiled. "No. Unfortunately, I hardly grew up with it." He took off his black, Rayban Sunglasses and polished them with a satin handkerchief. "This is going to sound like a poor little rich boy story ... And seldom do those receive commiserate ears." Wayne re-donned his sunglasses. "So let's rather savor these moments."

''No. Please." Lenore resumed holding his hands. "I'll understand. Tell me."

"Okay, I hardly grew-up in our Stanforth, Queen Anne

108

Mansion. And rarely did I enjoy this Victorian summer home. My parents shipped me off to Greenwich Academy in England. It was, for all intents and purposes, a Dickinesque orphanage with better-educated teachers. Captain Blye like school masters substituted for parents. Nine months out of the year, I lived four to a cell. I had only a steel bed and a pine writing table. My only clothes were school uniforms. At least the kids in Oliver Twist's workhouse wore comfortable rags. Our school uniforms were made of coarse chafing wool. And the tight, starched collars," Wayne scratched his neck. "Surely you can imagine that our school ties felt like a noose. Let one blotch, smudge, or stain besmirch your uniform," Wayne shook his head, "and your butt got a black and blue stain from a cane. Dickens managed to give the thieves raising Oliver Twist a benevolent touch. As far as I'm concerned, my schoolmasters amounted to nothing more than sadists wearing an academic fig leaf. Fail to make your bed at less than the Royal Navy standard, turn in what they regarded as a sloppy lesson, speak out of tum, look at them wrong, and they ... Let me put it to you this way, one of my classmates was named Turner Brown. Every time a schoolmaster called his name, I shrank."

Lenore chuckled; Wayne didn't.

"The physical environment of the place," Wayne continued, "including England's weather, featured as many shades of lead as the eye can fathom. And the food, talk about bland, even Oliver Twist wouldn't ask for more of that stuff. Remember that Charlie Chaplin movie about the Klondike?"

"You mean the one where they eat their shoes?"

''Exactly. Old Charlie would've had a harder time carving what they called 'Salisbury Steak'. "

"You got to go home on Christmas, didn't you?"

"Sure. For two weeks. At the height of the social season. Of course, my parents felt children were to be seen, not heard." Wayne spotted a small, broken conch shell half buried in the sand. He picked it up, covered his ear with it, then gave it to Lenore who likewise listen to its echo. Wayne continued: "WASP. That pejorative acronym might have some sting, if it expressed an underlying characteristic. A more effective slur would be sockeye"

"Sockeye?"

"Yes. Sockeye. The salmon that lays about two million eggs. The typical *WASP* parent cares about as much for their progeny as a sockeye salmon does for each of its two-million eggs. I know you've heard it before, although no one bothers listening, or gives what I'm about to say any credibility, but I'd have traded my fleeting moments at home, which usually consisted of dressing up in an adorable little suit, greeting the guests, letting them pinch your rosy little cheeks, then off to your little room with a servant enforcing silence. I'll trade that for a disadvantaged home that gave time and love their children."

"Surely it wasn't all that bad."

"Worse. I spared you the details of those many days away from home." Wayne picked up a clam shell and skipped it into the ocean. "Sports provided no relief Greenwich gave us a choice between rowing and cricket. Only an aspiring galley slave would chose rowing. Cricket? I don't know how many members of our Windsor Country Club have played the game of its namesake. Essentially cricket is baseball with two bases, a canoe paddle for a bat, and three sticks for a strike zone. Even if those games were to your liking, Greenwich sucked the fun right out of 'em. Hell, a sailor executed his duties on the Bounty under less regimentation than sports at Greenwich."

"Wayne. How did you ever? I mean, I hear what you're saying and all. But you're everything but a bland adult." Lenore hopped away from a comber. "How did you ever overcome such a drab and loveless childhood? A more passionate and caring man I've never met."

"I have faith that all things work together for the good. Even growing up at Greenwich Academy. Often they took us on field trips to England's great museums." Wayne allowed a wave to wash over his waterproof nylon hiking boots. "The color of Gauguin took me to warm and exotic lands. Through Toulouse-Lautrec I could imagine thrills beyond silence at six, lights out at nine. I gained a sensual passion from Rossetti that one better not find at a boys-only academy." Wayne chuckled. "Soon I even started seeing Greenwich Academy's otherwise dull terrain with a Constable or Turner perspective."

"Did Greenwich Academy teach you the piano?"

"Yes they did. And what a blessing! Mastering the works of Chopin, Mozart, Rachmaninoff, and Beethoven gave me a melodic break from the academy. Schubert's impromptu number 3 in G Flat Major ... I met a beautiful English girl at an academy dance. I highly chaperoned one, I might add. Anyway, I learned that piece just for her."

"You're making me jealous. You've never played it for me."

"I never got to play it for her either. Yet that wonderful melody still stirs my heart."

"Will you play it for me tonight?"

Wayne braced Lenore's shoulders. "I'd love to."

"Thank you." Lenore blushed and looked downward, breaking eye contact. "Um ... Didn't you say Wagner was your favorite? Can you play me something by him?"

Wayne chuckled. "I don't think so. For starters, it requires a hundred-piece orchestra. In addition to that, only about a hundred people in the world can sing Wagner at an acceptable level. And I'm certainly not one of the hundred. Maybe that's why I'll always remember the academy taking us to see and hear the entire Ring cycle. After that, I faced my school master's with Siegfried's fearlessness. Let the bastards cane me! One day I'd slay them with the sword *Notung."* Wayne swept an imaginary sword.

"I hardly think that an Oliver Twist workhouse could deliver such privileged, cultural enrichment."

"Touché." Wayne walked on without looking at Lenore. "I told you that nobody cares for poor little rich boy stories."

"No. No." Lenore spun in front of Wayne. "I understand. I do. Although I only attended Bohm School for Girls as a day student, I could always sense something lacking in even the wealthiest girls' lives. What about summer?" Lenore grabbed Wayne's arm. "Surely you spent summers here with your family?"

Not with family." Wayne marched forward, breaking Lenore's grip. "My parents sent me directly from Greenwich Academy in England to Camp Greenbrier in West Virginia." Wayne beamed. "A boy couldn't ask for a better summer than Camp

Greenbrier. It's nestled among mystic mountains and next to a crystal-clear river. And talk about fresh air! The aroma of the river or flora on the mountains was orgasmic. We played baseball and basketball for fun, shot white water rapids in canoes, and went on camping trips. But teenage councilors just weren't parents. One week. Just one week I spent here with my parents. If they weren't playing tennis or sunbathing," Wayne chuckled, "attempting to match the skin color of their disdained servants, they might spend some time with me. Invariably, I did not enjoy my precious Cape May week on the beach with my parents. I ended up cloistered in that loft painting seascapes." Wayne pointed to his mansion.

"You never told me you painted."

"Oops." Wayne covered his mouth. "I wanted to save that as a surprise. Tonight, the Endicotts, Argus Garvos, and some others are going to join us. I'm going to unveil my latest works. First I want to give you a private viewing."

"The Endicotts? Argus Garvos?" A pallid Lenore's eyes looked like a pair of freshly minted quarters. A vision of Lance and office cronies Pat Huggins, Eddie Krause, and Paul Barton guzzling bourbon and exchanging dirty jokes made her nibble her right ring finger. "Um, Thank you." Lenore extracted her finger and caught her breath. "I'm flattered. I, um, feel so privileged to see your works before such bigwigs."

"Bigwigs? Nonsense. They're our friends."

"Yes, of course. I was just thinking. Surely your paintings made your parents proud?"

Wayne sniggered. "Didn't I wish. Unfortunately, my parents failed to distinguish my mature oil paintings from my kindergarten finger paintings of red roosters."

Lenore blanched.

Wayne braced Lenore's shoulders. "Sure, as Hillary Sterling ever so eloquently put it to me the other day, the Suttons aren't the Madisons or Endicotts."

"What did Hillary Sterling say about me?" Lenore jerked her hands to her hips and hunched her shoulders.

"You really don't want to know. Relax." Wayne took both of Lenore's hands. "I put her in her place. And rest assured she's uninvited from tonight's get-together. I told her that you, like Dorothy, possessed something far richer than old money." Wayne squeezed her hands tighter and looked directly into her eyes. "You had the love of a family." Hearts pounding with the pulse of the crashing breakers, their heads approached.

Suddenly a seagull shat on Lenore's jacket.

"Ugh," she groaned at the puke green splatter. Two

earthbound seagull's squawked at her. She saw them transmogrify into chickens. Their fowl heads now took on Betty Kirby and Hillary Sterling's foul visages.

"Manicure. Hairdo. Lenore stinks of chicken do," the Betty Kirby chicken clucked. "Temporary insanity. Insane with grief over his dead wife. He's only seeing you on the rebound," the Hillary Sterling chicken clucked.

"Manicure. Hairdo. Lenore stinks of chicken do." The Betty Kirby chicken continued her taunt.

"You're nothing but a common, vulgar, chicken farm redneck slob," said the Hillary Sterling Chicken. "As soon as he gets over Dorothy, he'll realize this. Then he'll dump you."

"Manicure. Hairdo. Lenore stinks of chicken do."

"You' re just the first available live body for him to project his dead wife into," the Hillary Sterling chicken continued. "And what about your body? Tonight, you'll meet Argus Garvos's girlfriend. That kind of body you'll soon have to compete against. Ha! Ha! Ha!"

"Ha! Ha! Ha!, Ha! Ha! Ha!" The Betty Kirby chicken also guffawed.

Lenore lurched backward. Her expression resembled that of a Voodoo doll.

"Oh well, looks like we ran into a mischievous little gull, didn't we?" Wayne stepped forward. He removed Lenore's jacket, folded it, and placed it on the beach. Next, he draped his coat over her shoulders.

As they embraced and kissed, she saw two decapitated chickens running madly. Hillary Sterling and Betty Kirby's bird-sized heads clucked harmlessly in the sand.

Myles watched from a second-story balcony. He bit his lower lip hard enough to draw blood.

* * *

Fullerton Endicott edged in a plush velvet, Victorian antique chair. Fireplace flames cast amber beams across his crystal cognac snifter. Yet the fireplace was cooler than a polar bear den compared to his blistering rebuke of unruly, protesting students. Even hotter sparked the two-two-thousand-volt seat that he suggested strapping the instigators into. His wife and oldest son had joined Argus Garvos and his forty-years younger girlfriend, *Playboy Magazine's* 'Miss April', in Wayne's art studio.

"This one you must exhibit professionally." Elizabeth Endicott sipped sherry imported from Andalusia, Spain. "My son," she placed her hand on Marion's shoulder, "is debuting his latest project in a couple of months. We'll gladly include this painting in the exhibition."

"Thank you anyway." Wayne stepped in front of his painting. "But seascapes are currently unfashionable. Besides, my art is only a hobby. It would look mundane next to Marion's professional virtuosity."

"Modesty. Modesty." Marion turned to Wayne with dilating pupils. "I should be the one worried about getting upstaged."

"Astute statement, Marion," Wayne replied. "Often your mother has told me of the professional art world's immense competitive pressure. That, and worrying about public and expert opinion, I can do without. Rather my art remain personal and therapeutic, my means of maintaining inner peace."

''Now who's the one making astute statements." Marion gently moved Wayne away from his painting. "You may say that seascapes are out of vogue. But since the dawn of time, man has sought the sea for her soothing effect. As you know," Marion's eyelashes fluttered as he turned to Wayne. "The most fundamental step in the artistic process is arranging your picture's objects or figures. That action determines not only your composition's ability to please the eye, but also the efficacy of its emotional impact. A symmetrical or balanced composition will look calm, while an unbalanced scene can be disturbing. Sure. Many of art's greatest works are quite upsetting. I can tell though, that you intended this painting to portray an air of calm and tranquility." Marion pointed to the center of Wayne's painting. "I see that you've arranged the principal scene around a bisecting rainbow. Fab-u-lous!" Marion grabbed Elizabeth by the arm and pulled her closer. "Ma ma." He pointed to the painting. "Can you see how this rainbow combines with his ship's mast to divide the picture into two equal parts between the dark ship and the silvery sea? By dividing your picture in the center, Wayne, you've achieved perfect symmetry. Con-grat-u-la-tions." With two hands, Marion squeezed Wayne's right hand and looked directly into his eyes.

Wayne flinched from his grip.

"Mission accomplished!" Marion flapped his right hand, then clasped Wayne's left hand. "Your painting truly achieves calm and tranquility."

Wayne nervously pulled back his hand and slipped it into his cardigan pocket.

Elizabeth linked Wayne and Marion by bracing a hand on each of their shoulders. "Marion's right. You must let me exhibit this, so others can benefit."

"Thanks. Liz. Nice thought. But anyway, the public can't really appreciate ... "

"Oh, Wayne." *Miss April* stepped forward. The sixty-year-old European mining magnate's girlfriend wore a white leather halter top with black tassels. Not that anyone looking in her direction would take note of the black tassels. Her bared abdomen boasted angles firm enough to bump a Babylonian belly dancer into the Tigris River. Clad in the era's latest fad, a mini skirt, her legs looked like Parthenon columns with cowboy boots acting as base and plinth. "Won't you paint me riding sidesaddle on a white horse?" She turned her head, spraying a Niagara Falls of blond hair.

Lenore pushed aside 'Miss April.' "Maybe later." Lenore braced Wayne's hand and shoulder and directed him toward the dining room. "I think Mr. Sokamoto is ready to serve dinner."

* * *

Wayne Madison's invited guests gathered around a hibachi. First a kimono clad waitress served a unique appetizer.

"It looks like fishing bait!" Myles pointed. "Actually it's Sushi." Wayne answered.

"Sushi is divine." Marion interjected. "Yes. It's raw fish, but it tastes mag-ni-fi-co."

"Raw fish? P.U. Yech." Myles pulled his face.

"Awww…young man," Wayne replied. "You like steak, don't you? Wait until you taste the beef teriyaki. Mr. Sakamoto will prepare it right before your eyes."

"Umm... Yes." Elizabeth Endicott nibbled an uncooked tidbit. "This Sushi piece's flavor is divine."

"I like it too," 'Miss April' added. "But rather than fish, it tastes more like Kentucky Fried Chicken without the crust."

Lenore blanched.

"You won't get me to eat that raw fish stuff" Myles replied.

Wayne turned to the brat. "Well here comes something I think you'll enjoy."

The kimono clad waitress walked five paces behind the chef.

She placed a domed silver tray on a stand adjacent to the hibachi. Lifting the lid, she revealed a succulent array of beef cubes, chopped onions, and sweet and tangy sauces.

Mr. Sokamoto looked more like a conductor sweeping and waving his baton to an orchestra than a chef slicing and stirring food before a brat. The chef grinned and bowed after scooping Myles his helping.

The brat tacitly said '*You're crazy*' by wryly curling his lip. Myles soon took a narrow, pointed, lacquered chopstick in each hand. He started to lift a bite to his mouth. "Splash." His beef belly-flopped into his plate's sauce.

"Ahh ... Eating with chopsticks is an art form in itself" Wayne took the chopsticks from Myles and helped him with the proper one handed, thumb and forefinger grip.

"So what? I wanna eat with a fork."

Wayne sighed. The waitress smiled and handed Myles a fork.

Marion politely returned chef Sokamoto's bow. Elizabeth raised her chin and nodded approval after her turn. Fullerton growled during the chef's performance, yet still thanked him.

*Miss April* pointed. "Wow! Look at him go!" Afterward, Argus held her hand and guided a chop sticked portion to her mouth.

Mitchell Endicott swallowed his morsel of beef. "Wayne. What a splendid treat. Not only is the food delicious but our chef put on a great show." He smiled. "I thank you."

Estelle sat next to her older brother. "I'll second that. Thank you so much Mr. Madison."

"You're welcome, Estelle. But I'd say that you earned it." Wayne smiled at her. "Your new youth committee is already paying dividends to the community. Great job."

Estelle blushed. "Thank you again Mr. Madison."

Myles then interrupted. "Hey look everybody! I'm a

walrus!" Chopped sticks jammed up nostrils, He brandished his new tusks.

The socialite gathering gasped, groaned, or murmured. Lenore fought her bladder to a draw.

* * *

Unlike his committed older brother, who would've gotten locked in a closet, Myles was sent to a large sea-facing bedroom for the rest of the evening. Shortly after the guests departed, his mother visited him. "I want you to learn the importance of proper behavior. What did you think of Estelle?

Myles didn't answer.

"I know she's a few years older than you, but I'm sure you noticed how radiant she looked. She's also poised and confident. I hope someday that you'll meet a girl like her. When you do, I know that you will want to make a good impression on her parents." Lenore looked into his eyes. "You know that what you did tonight made you look bad with her parents.

"No Mommy. "Myles held Lenore's hand. "I don't want no girl. I only love you." Myles hugged his mother.

"I love you too Myles."

Lenore turned out the lights and closed the door behind her.

Soon all of the lights dimmed. Predictably, a half-hour later the brat wandered to his mother's bedroom. He clasped the door knob and turned. Locked! Then he heard a frightful sound. Squeaking bed springs! Myles's heart fell from his thorax like a trapeze artist from his perch. It bounced up from his stomach as a fiery lava clump. "You whore!" He yelled and banged on the door. "You fuckin' whore! You dirty fucking whore!"

Lenore sprang from her bed and bolted open the door.

Instantly the brat noticed her empty bed. "Mommy!" He bawled and clung to his mother. "It's all right, honey. It's all right." Lenore returned the embrace and patted his back. She glanced at a perplexed Wayne Madison standing at the end of the corridor. Her jaw chattered before deciding to take Myles to her bed.

# Chapter 12

With a dentist's probe, Geoffrey speared a small triangular, balsa wood fin and carefully glued it to his rocket's cardboard fuselage. Stage one complete! Admiringly, he sat back and gazed upon his handiwork.

"Good morning Geoffrey." Dr. Tryvye entered the boy's room. "Another model rocket I see." The psychiatrist perused the aerodynamic cardboard cylinders with balsa fins and nose cones. "Tell me Geoffrey. Do you more enjoy erecting them or launching them?"

"Both. Will you take me outside and fly them with me?"

"We'll see. We'll see." The psychiatrist jutted his head. "Launching your rockets is fun for me too."

"Ya! I like it most when they fly to their highest, then the parachute pops out!"

"Hmm," the psychiatrist pinched his chin. "Ahh," he jotted notes into a clipboard. "But first you have a very welcome visitor."

"A Visitor?"

"Yes ... "

A white-uniformed nurse gently rapped on the open door and

nodded. "Yes." Dr. Tryvye pointed to the doorway. "Send him in."

"Geoffrey!" The visitor spread his arms.

The boy stood and gawked at him in shock. "Granddad? You came to see me?"

"Why of course." Scotch put his hand on the door frame. He smiled upon the realization that, however pale his grandson's complexion, he looked healthy. "You didn't think I'd desert you, did you?" Although Geoffrey looked back at him through hazy eyes, Scotch saw them as two windows to an inner air deeper than most adolescents. The boy commanded a presence of gained maturity, however, Scotch also sensed a loss. Nevertheless, how can one lose what he never had?

The boy's vision remained fuzzy. "Is it really you? Even mom won't visit me. She hasn't even phoned."

"You have to understand. Your mother ... "

"She's convinced I did It! Isn't she?" An angry tear sprayed from Geoffrey's eye. "Just about everybody thinks I did it!" Geoffrey shook his fists. "But Jesus knows," Geoffrey sobbed, "Jesus knows I didn't do it. And Aunt Lizzie. She believes me. But nobody else does."

Scotch smiled relief at the boy's outburst. At least it revealed that missing shred of child in his grandson. "Well, I know that you could never kill anybody. I'm going to prove it and get you out of here."

"That's what Aunt Lizzie says. But I'm still stuck here."

"But isn't here a lot better than where you were?"

"Ya." Geoff covered his eyes. "I am grateful that I'm no longer down there. I thought they'd keep me down below forever. But I prayed and prayed ... "

"Your faith worked then, didn't it? Now here you are safe and comfortable. So, you gotta keep that faith Norman taught you."

"Norman? He don't believe me about Norman." Geoff pointed at Dr. Tryvye.

The shrink balked.

"He doesn't believe in Jesus either." Scotch winked at the psychiatrist. "But your Lord took pretty darn good care of you, didn't he?"

"Yes." Geoff sniffled. "The pit was still such an awful place. I don't think about it anymore when I'm awake. But whenever I sleep," he looked at Scotch with teary eyes, "I have terrible nightmares. Why did he," anger returning, Geoff again pointed at Dr. Tryvye, "keep me down there for so long? I didn't do nothin' to deserve it."

The psychiatrist jotted into his clipboard.

"Well isn't he your friend now?" Scotch nodded at the shrink.

"Ya I guess so. He talks nicer to me and he plays rockets with me." Dr. Tryvye smiled.

"So now with everything getting better, can't you see that the next step is getting you home completely?"

"Home? Mom doesn't want me no more." Geoffrey sat and dropped his elbows to knees, burying face in palms.

"Well Grandma and I want ya!" Scotch pumped his fist. "As soon as we get ya outta here, you can come live with us on the farm!"

The surprised boy looked up. "Do you mean that?"

"Have I ever lied to you?"

Geoff's vision crystallized.

"So start thinking of the farm as your home!" Scotch spread his arms.

"Awww ... Granddad." The boy ran over and hugged Scotch. "So you believe me then?"

"Of course I do." Scotch patted the boy's back.

"But he," Geoffrey returned his attention to Dr. Tryvye, "still thinks I'm lying. Even about Norman." Scotch grinned foxlike. "Does he now?" The Grandfather nodded at the door.

Clad in a clean, pressed blue suit topped by a Naval captain's hat, Geoffrey's best friend hopped in.

"Norman!" The boy ran to the old man and hugged him.

"Howdy there Geoffrey!" Norman patted his back. "I'm just as happy to see you too. Wish it wasn't here but have faith. You ain't gonna be in this place much longer."

"Who on Earth is he?" Eduardo Tryvye, looking at Scotch, pointed to Norman. "How did he get in here?"

"Dr. Tryvye. I proudly present you Apostle, I mean, Mister, Norman Bell."

The psychiatrist lowered his half-eye spectacles to the tip of his Byzantine nose. He stood still as Dracula duped into witnessing dawn.

"Why God-Bless ya doctor." Norman clasped and shook Eduardo's limp hand. "I heard so much about ya." He cuffed the psychiatrist's shoulder. "You helpin' Geoffrey get through this thing the Bible call a tribulation. And thank you for buyin' my friend all these nice books, and model cars, boats, airplanes, and rockets."

"No Norman." Geoffrey interjected. "Aunt Lizzie brought

them."

"Aunt Lizzie?" Scotch scratched his brow. "Who is this Aunt Lizzie?"

"She's this real nice lady. She visits me all the time and brings me all these cool presents . . ."

"Ruff. Ruff." Suddenly a small brown mongrel with a vertical white blaze bisecting his face padded to the boy.

Geoffrey squatted, allowing the mutt to lick his face. "Awww ... Who's he?"

"Why that's Chester A. Dawg," Norman announced. "Right now he's living with us. But as soon as ya get outta here, he's your dog."

"Sasha must not like sharing the shack with a dog. And doesn't he chase the other cats?"

"Geoffrey!" Norman beamed radiantly as a tropical sun. "Sasha and me don't live in the shack no more. We all live at your granddaddy's farm!" Geoffrey turned to Scotch. He grinned and nodded.

"Ya see," Norman continued, "your grand-daddy gave me a job! I help fix things around the farm. Plus, two times each day I feed and water the chickens. I also clean their cages. Some may say that's dirty work. But you know I always say that all work is honorable. A man can take pride in doin' any job well. Even if it only is shinin' shoes or cleanin' after chickens. But for doin' my duties on your granddad's farm, I make better money than shinin' shoes, and, I earn my stay in the guest house. It's got heat, electricity, and runnin' hot and cold water. Sasha lives in there with me. The other cats live in the barn. Sasha's still the boss. Only instead of protectin' me, they protect the chickens from foxes, weasels, and hawks. Soon you can join us, and we'll all be one big happy family."

"But will you, I don't know, but will you ... "

"Ol' Norman knows what you're a wantin' to ask me. Will I still be the same ol' Norman? Of course. Hey, on my days off, I ride the bus back to the ol' train tracks for my long thinkin' walks. If ya call what I do walkin' ." Norman tapped his bad leg and chuckled. "And I ain't planin' on cleanin' after chickens forever. Your Grand-dad's foreman's talkin' 'bout movin' on. When that day comes, I'm hopin' to take his place."

"But I thought you always said that money and material things didn't matter."

"I never said they don't matter. I said they ain't what matters most. What matters most is givin' your all to God and the ability he gave ya. And you know I always told ya that God gave you lots' of that. Sometimes ya gotta ask yourself, is what I'm doin' now gonna matter a hundred years from today? Well, settin' a good example to a smart young man like you is gonna matter in a hundred years, fo-sure. And doin' no work but shinin' shoes for people I hope will give me more than I really earned, ain't gonna do it. I maybe didn't complain much about eatin' nothin but oatmeal and beans, but how do ya think I got even that food? Not by stealin'. That's fo-sure."

Geoffrey's face froze with delight. Tears welled in his eyes. He ran over and again hugged his friend.

"Ruff. Ruff." Chester A Dawg braced his forepaws on the boy's leg. "And him too." Scotch added.

The dog soon padded to Norman "Chester's a great dog." Norman petted the panting dog atop his head. "But I know you're still sad about Yogi. Me too. But Yogi, he's now happy up there in dog heaven. So, I'm sure he wants ya to love Chester just as much as ya can."

"Awww ... Yes. I will."

"Well, you gots to. 'Cause a dog only gets one life down here on Earth. But a cat's different. They get nine lives. I want to reintroduce one that wants to spend a few of hers with you. Psssh, psssh, come on in girl."

Watching the next occurrence, Geoffrey felt detached, as if viewing a television news clip. A fluffy white cat bounced into the room.

Geoffrey breathlessly watched her approach.

The cat pounced into his arms. "Meow." Geoffery's mouth dropped, his thoughts froze. "It's, it's, it's ... Lee Lee!" Geoffrey hugged the cat, kissed her forehead, then copiously cried. "Lee Lee! Lee Lee! Lee Lee!"

"Ruff! Ruff!" Chester barked.

"Chester A. Dawg will be a waitin' for ya at the farm," Norman said. "But 'till then, Lee Lee's gonna stay here with ya and help make ya stay more bearable."

"Now wait just a minute." Dr. Tryvye prodded at Norman. "I, not you, determine Harlond State's policy. Just allowing those animals in the building for an ephemeral visit amounted to manifestly unorthodox procedure. And how does Mr. Sutton show his gratitude? By executing a subterfuge-- smuggling you in. So, when you and Mr. Sutton conclude your visit, that cat, and the dog, all four of you that matter, will return to the farm."

"Ya bent your rules and let Geoffrey's pets in. Why?"

"Well, um, I based my decision upon the analytical realization ... "

"I don't much understand the words you say." Norman spread his arms. "But I do understand what you mean. You let the dog and cat in the building just to see the boy happy. Deep inside you really are a very nice man."

"Hmm ... " The psychiatrist pinched his goatee. "Ahh ... " He pointed to the ceiling. "My decision, reasoned from a scientific appraisal, based upon empirical evidence, is that caring for a pet is manifestly therapeutic to a disturbed patient."

"You mean I can keep her?" Geoffrey's face lit up like a jack-o'-lantern.

"Yes. You can keep her." The psychiatrist ruffled his hair. "But I'm making it your responsibility to feed her and clean her box everyday."

"All right!" Geoffrey held Lee Lee cheek to cheek. "Of course I'll take good care of my Lee Lee cat. Thank you doctor."

"Meow." Lee Lee mewed her gratitude to the psychiatrist.

"Come on you guys." Scotch looked at his watch. "The days are short. Let's go outside while we still have daylight. Do you want to launch your rockets? Sail your boats in the pond? Or play some baseball?"

"Baseball sounds like fun," Geoffrey answered. "And we sure won't get too many more warm days like this until spring. But we don't have enough players."

"Oh yes we do!" Scotch beamed. "Eric and Howard are waiting in the lobby."

"Eric and Howard!"

"Yup! Eric and Howard. Come on let's go."

* * *

Scotch squatted and pounded his catcher's mitt.

Norman, balancing himself on his crutch, tapped a plastic dinner plate acting as home plate with his cane. He then poised his cane like a baseball bat.

"Give 'em your knuckler!" Scotch shouted.

Geoffrey's spin-free pitch bobbed and weaved past Norman, plopping into his grandfather's glove.

"What?" Norman muttered

"Ste-e-e-e-rike!" Geoffrey pumped his fist.

"Hey, let me tell ya sumptin' there Geoffrey. Ole Satchel threw about a hundred times harder, but I ain't never seen nothin' dance around like that pitch!"

"Hey!" Dr. Tryvye picked up a baseball bat. "It's my turn! My turn. I want a try!" The psychiatrist bumped Norman aside. Dr.

Tryvye, gripping a real baseball bat with hands several inches apart, fecklessly chopped at Geoffrey's next pitch. "No fair! No fair!" The psychiatrist dumped his bat and flapped his hands. "You're not allowed to make your pitch drop like that!"

Eric ran in. "Bet I can hit it."

"Okay Geoffrey!" Scotch pounded his mitt. "Here's your big test. You know that he's the starting left-fielder for The Harland School."

Eric dug in his rear foot. Twice he slowly, threateningly half-swung, like a minute man priming his musket. Then he coiled his bat.

Geoff pushed an undulating pitch in his direction.

The high school baseball player imitated a statue as he watched Geoff's delivery float by.

Scotch caught in his glove the pitch slow enough to snatch with his bare hand. "Strike called!" He slyly looked up to Eric. "Want to try again?"

"That's only one." Eric answered. "I get two more tries."

Eric fanned on the next pitch, twisting himself like a corkscrew. Scotch held the ball up to Eric. "Sure you want to try again?"

"Shut up and catch, old man! I'll do the hitting, thank you."

Eric strode into the next pitch. His eyes opened wide at the beach ball looking delivery. He sprung his bat. The pitch radically veered to the left. Harland School's left-fielder stopped his swing.

The pitch bounced away from the catcher, rolling to Norman. He scooped it up. "You went around." The old man pointed at Eric. "You swung. That's strike three."

Eric sighed, then bit his lip. He leaned on his bat and said: "I don't know where you learned to throw pitches like that, but whenever we play again, you're on my team."

"Eric." Scotch slapped his back. "Hit Geoff and your brother some fungos. I want to talk to Dr. Tryvye."

* * *

A midst the sound of horsehide buffeting ash and leather, invigorated young voices, and a joyful old one shouting encouragement, Scotch addressed the psychiatrist. "How can you still suspect that boy of patricide?"

"Inside these walls dwell even calmer and exoterically sound individuals, culpable and capable of far worse."

"You've got to be kidding."

"I can introduce you to Miss Rosie Garett. Remember her?

The nursery school teacher who laced her infant charges' milk and cookies with ... "

"Yes. I know of Rosie Garett. And no. I most surely, *manifestly*," Scotch scratched his neck, "don't want to meet her."

"Then you manifestly understand why Geoffrey must stay."

"Sure. I wish you could release him as soon as possible. But I do realize that the situation is more tangled than that. I do have a suggestion that can start unraveling the web. First, I hope you recognize just how well Geoffrey's coped with his severe ordeals."

"Yes, Mr. Sutton. I am impressed with his internal reaction to his acute stressors."

"Second, I apologize for tricking you into meeting Norman. When we have more time," Scotch chuckled, "I'll explain just how I got my nickname in the first place. Nevertheless, he represents yet another piece of Geoffrey's testimony that you rejected but is now confirmed."

"Yes. Yes." Dr. Tryvye spoke through clenched teeth. "What is your objective?"

"My objective is to establish that the boy's telling the truth."

"Mr. Sutton. I am a psychiatrist. I yielded a deference to your legal expertise. Please grant the same to my psychiatric education.

Lying and deceit inflict a great deal of stress upon the normal psyche. One objective of my training is the cultivation of an awareness to the outward manifestations of this inner stress, both in verbal and body language. In my extensive observation of the patient, I have yet detected any of the outward manifestations of prevarication."

"Sounds to me as if we are yet another step closer."

"Not necessarily Mr. Sutton. I said a normal psyche. My initial diagnosis of the patient determined that he suffers from a borderline personality disorder. BFDs characteristically display a maddening ignorance to the consequences of their actions. Often BPD's will justify, or, even believe, their own deceptions, thus eliminating the outward manifestations of their devious behavior."

Scotch turned and faced him. "My idea will take us a giant leap forward. I am proposing an objective and disinterested test. I am confident enough in Geoffrey's innocence to submit him to a polygraph exam."

"A polygraph exam?" The psychiatrist turned to Scotch. "You're a lawyer. You should know better. Polygraph results are inadmissible in court."

"Admissible as evidence, no. Helpful, yes. Polygraph results, in a nutshell, Dr. Tryvye, are sometimes extremely accurate.

The military especially holds them in high esteem. The results are inadmissible mainly to protect the accused from the prosecution. Nevertheless, often police forces will redirect an investigation if a result vindicates a suspect."

"Ya. Ya. What you are saying I am manifestly aware of"

"Perhaps then, Dr. Tryvye, such a result will lead you to an *analytical realization*."

"An analytic realization, hmm." The psychiatrist pinched his goatee. Ahh." He pointed upward. "No analytic insight can harm the codification of my scientific cognification of a patient's psychiatric dysfunction. We have the facilities here at the hospital. I can determine no reason not to test the boy. You will have the results before your visit next week. Nevertheless, the findings of such a coldly impartial judge may manifest dire repercussions to yourself."

"What are you saying?" Scotch asked.

"Hmm..Ahh…I see that you deny even the possibility of your grandson's guilt. Do you also realize that the loss of a father has manifested not an atom of grief in Geoffrey?"

"Many children are victims of dysfunctional parents. That such parents fail to establish love bonds with their children does not necessarily make the child incapable of love, or capable of murder."

"Agreed, Mr. Sutton. Nevertheless, the boy has manifested

no contrition over his father's murder. That fact bears no consequence if he is innocent of the crime, of course. But what if the polygraph exam proves that Geoffrey is lying, Mr. Sutton? You will then have to face the fact that your seemingly innocent grandson is a remorseless killer."

# Chapter 13

Lenore strummed her fingers on the kitchen table. She stared at the phone, hoping willpower alone would make it ring. Even the noise of the Japanese monster flick that Myles was watching on TV failed to distract her. One week. An entire week! Still no word from Wayne.

"Ring!"

Her face lit up like a torch. She grabbed the receiver before the second ring. "Yes." Time halted.

"Lenore?"

A female voice. Lenore dropped her head. "It's Dolores. Next Friday at eight, I'm hosting a dinner party at my place. I still can't reach Wayne. But surely you two will come..."

"Come on Godzilla! Kill 'em all! Kill 'em all!"

Lenore plugged her free ear with a finger. "I can't hear you, Dolores."

"My dinner party." Dolores added a pique of petulance to her voice. "You and Wayne will ..."

"Go Godzilla! Go! That's it! Pick up the bus and smash every damn one of 'em! Yeah!" Myles clapped.

"Your place sounds like a madhouse."

"It's just my little boy playing. Children. You understand?"

"Kick the train over! Kick the damn train over! Yeah! All right! That'll show 'em!"

"Wayne and I will be happy to attend your dinner party. See you Friday." Lenore slammed down the phone then marched into the lounge. "Myles!" She prodded. "When I'm on the phone, you will not make any noise!"

"If you're talking to Wayne Madison, I will." Myles grinned.

Lenore glared at her gloating son. She saw something deeper. An evil perhaps? His smile teased her. *'Yes! He's teasing me!'* She tried to block out 12-year-old Betty Norton. *"Manicure, hairdo, Lenore smells like chicken do."* Toys, candy wrappers, and soda cans were scattered about the room. An overturned popcorn bowl, its greasy kernels had embedded themselves into the carpet. Myles's visage continued to taunt. *'It's his fault that I no longer have a maid.' 'Wayne..Wayne...Wayne'*...Living with Lance and his filth ... *Wayne Madison: obedient servants, luxurious home* ...chocolate now driveled down her son's chin ... She spotted a plastic Wiffleball bat... She snatched it and slugged Myles's head like Dick Allen on a hanging curveball.

The shocked brat wavered between semiconscious oblivion

and conscious agony... He conceived himself suspended by the feet, inside a bell. He acted as bell hammer. A tuxedoed Wayne Madison stood above. His left hand dangled a two-foot-high version of his mother in a wedding dress. "Bang! Bang!" Myles's head struck metal walls as Wayne's right hand rocked the bell. The brat's head felt like a boulder tumbling down a granite slope, his skull an avalanche of clangor... He scrunched into a fetal position and squeezed his temples.

"You spoilt little bastard!" Lenore, *whiffle* ball bat at side, stood over him. "You cleanup this mess, Now! Then go to your room!" Lenore prodded. "And no T.V.!"

Myles looked at her through hazy eyes. After three snorting breaths, he saw Wayne Madison laughing at him. "Fuck You! Whore!"

"Hghhh." Lenore recoiled the bat.

Myles sprung to his feet and seized the yellow plastic bat. He turned and whacked his mother's breasts.

A shrieking Lenore cupped her nipples and fell.

"Whore! Whore! Whore!" Those epithets punctuated each ensuing blow to her ribs.

She gasped and flopped on the floor like a boated fish.

With two hands, Myles cocked the bat over his head. "You fuckin' bitch!" He thrust it down on her.

Lenore lay still as the weapon bounced off her back and dribbled across the carpet. The brat hunched his shoulders and jutted his head. "Whore!" He turned and sprinted away..

Lenore could only listen to her son galloping up the stairs and slaming the bedroom door. '*Just another tenttrum.*' Soon she stumbled into the kitchen. Seeing the dormant telephone felt worse than if Myles's plastic bat were hickory. Lenore lay on her stomach and cried into her hands. The telephone remained silent.

# Chapter 14

Dr. Tryvye unlocked Geoffrey's door and entered. "It's time."

The boy placed his Bible on the desk and bravely rose. Two burly guards flanked his psychiatrist, one a middle linebacker-sized Black man with a permanent scowl; the other a White man with cauliflower ears and broken nose.

"Don't worry. I won't make you wear a straight jacket. Mr. Washington and Mr. Vitale will assure your behavior. Not that you've ever acted disorderly since arriving at your new home, it's procedure, you understand?"

"Yes. I understand." The boy spoke through a constricted throat. "You're not scared, are you?"

"No." Geoffrey told his day's first lie.

"Well, you have no need for fear." Dr. Tryvye secured a clipboard under his arm. "I am submitting you to nothing more than a test of self-realization. I cannot overemphasize that Harland State is a place of treatment. If our little examination extrapolates that you did indeed murder your father, we will still regard it as a gain. We can then redirect your therapy to mollify the deleterious manifestations of repressing your traumatic deed into your subconscious. Once we unearth this phenomenon from your inner mind, we can further alleviate the insalubrious manifestations of denial. You will soon gain crucial insights of self-awareness. Eventually, your ego will be able to contend with a less troublesome Id and Superego. Then you can ..."

"I told you a thousand times!" Geoffrey interrupted. "I didn't kill my father! I never killed in my life."

"Ah, ah, ah," the psychiatrist prodded. "Today you will testify not to me, will you now? A machine will act as impartial judge and jury. Come along. Let's not make the technician wait."

Geoff's body felt like a helium balloon while his feet seemed cast in lead. He fought the urge to keel over and retch. His formidable escort braced his arms, directing Geoff to his destination. They entered a chamber with only a bare pine chair and a machine sitting atop a table. The device had an array of wires, lights, and transistors. The white-smocked, bespectacled polygraph examiner looked tiny compared to the guards.

"Your examiner's name is Mr. Smith." Dr. Tryvye grasped Geoffrey's shoulder and pointed to the technician. "That should be easy enough for you to remember. Come along."

Guards Washington and Vitale led the boy to the chair and started strapping him in.

"I apologize for the bindings. Procedure. A polygraph examination can prove highly distressing. Many patients react unpredictably." Dr. Tryvye nodded to Mr. Smith.

He attached the electrodes to the boy's fingertips. Additionally, he wrapped a fabric band around his chest to monitor his heartbeat. "Hi Geoffrey. I am going to ask you a series of questions. Answer each query yes or no. My machine will measure your stress level. An abnormal stress level is an indication of deception. Do you understand?"

Geoffrey nodded.

"You will answer my questions with a simple yes or no, Geoffrey. Do you understand?"

"Yes."

"Very good. The first question. Is your name Geoffrey Burkett?"

"Yes."

"Are you thirteen-years-old?"

"Yes." A bead of sweat formed on his brow.

"On the day in question, did you attack your father with a chair?"

"Yes." Geoffrey mumbled.

"Yes or No. Speak up."

"Yes." Two lines of perspiration ran down Geoffrey's cheek. "Afterwards, did you murder your father with an ax?"

"I never killed nobody! How many times do I have to say it?"

"Yes or no?" Mr. Smith calmly asked.

"No! No! No!"

Dr. Tryvye rested thumb on chin and forefinger on cheek as he viewed the machine's undulating needles.

# Chapter 15

Lenore paced her kitchen floor like a lioness waiting her turn on the Colosseum floor. "Oh please call." She dropped into a chair and slumped her head on the kitchen table. "Oh God, make him call!" She pounded the tabletop.

"Mommy! Look at the football I won." Myles barged through the backdoor. "My gym teacher named me best player in the class." The brat stuffed the football into her gut much like his father would to Sly Horton at Franklin Field all those years ago.

"That's lovely, honey." Lenore didn't look at the ball.

"You don't care!"

"Of course I do, honey ..."

"Ring!"

Lenore leaped and snatched the phone receiver. "Hello?"

"Lenore. It's me."

She clutched her chest and fell back in her chair. "Sorry, I haven't phoned in a while ..."

"I got the prize because I scored more touchdowns than any of the other boys. I ..."

Lenore wedged the receiver between her shoulder and ear.

She frowned at her son and waved him out the back door with a jabbing motion.

Myles turned in a huff. He heard his mother say "Wayne" before he slammed the door behind him.

"I've got a great idea for us over Christmas week ..."

"You want to spend Christmas with me?" Both the edges of her lips and the pitch of her voice rose.

"Of course. Who else?"

Lenore stood. She felt herself float toward Heaven.

Bash! Bash! Clang! Clang! "Da, da, da da; da da da da da, da!" Crashing two metal trash can lids like cymbals, Myles reentered vocalizing the University of Pennsylvania's fight song, 'Hurrah for the Red and the Blue.'

"I can't even hear myself over all that racket."

"Huh." Lenore groaned and dropped the receiver. Scanning the kitchen, she quickly found the solution. She lunged over to the stove and grasped the metal soup spoon. With an overhand, whirlwind motion, she smashed it between her son's eyes. Myles staggered back. His trash can lids fell to the floor and clamored into the kitchen cabinets. "Ponk! Ponk!" Lenore struck his forehead twice.

Electric pitchforks of pain clouded Myle's vision. *'She's going to strike again.' I see Wayne Madison. He'e egging her on!'* Myles stood and charged the illusion of Wayne. He jammed his shoulder into his mother's ribs. Myles never looked up. "Madison!" Myles twirled punches and connected on the face that he thought belonged to his rival.

Lenore reacted to the spray of punches by spiking an elbow into her son's spine. He fell to his knees, paralyzed by the pain. She dragged him by the hair: out of the kitchen, through the dining room, and up the stairs. Seconds after reaching the upstairs hallway, she gained an epiphany. Her ultimate solution. Lenore pitched her younger son into the linen closet and locked the door. She then scurried into her bedroom and scooped up the spare phone. "Sorry for the interruption. Myles and some school friends were playing *Nerf* football in the lounge. They knocked over some furniture and made quite a commotion, didn't they? Don't worry. I sent them outside."

* * *

A scream rose in Myles's throat, but the darkness gagged him. *'Monsters!'* He couldn't see them or hear them. But he sensed their presence. *'They're going to punish me.'* He collapsed into the rear wall and cautiously slid onto his butt; he drew his knees into his chest and wept. Pinching shut his eyelids, he at last saw light specks.- *'Monster eyes!'* Their stench of death cloyed the air. He then saw a tall and slender Black man standing over him with his hands on his hips. "Deep inside, you know what you should do."

"Shut up! Shut up!" Myles shouted. "Go away!"

* * *

"Well, now that we have some quiet, I thought I'd ask you what you'd think about me flying us to Puerto Rico in my plane. From the airport we'll roll down to the Caribbean coast in an open jeep. Then what would you think about sailing with me on the phosphorous bay, in my racing sloop?"

"What would I think!" Lenore's face lit up like a torch. *'Keep your cool. Keep your cool.'* She steeled herself with three deep breaths and sat. "Wayne, aren't you ironic. What would I *think?* Well, you surely do leave me with some hard thinking at that. After all, you haven't called in ten days.

"I do have obligations as a committee member, you know. And spending Christmas with you in the Caribbean? That is quite a leap in our relationship."

"Have I ever acted any less than a perfect gentleman? I'm asking you to sail with me on my sloop, not..."

"It's not that. It's just..."

"Just what?"

"First let me look at my calendar... Elizabeth Endicott asked me personally to chair..."

"I'll talk to Liz. I'm sure she'll..."

"No. No." Lenore bit her lip and wrung the receiver. "Um, I mean, um, let me talk to her. I'm sure Hillary Sterling can sub for me. That still leaves next Thursday's Junior League auction. That one I do have to think about..."

* * *

He thought of a coffin. Myles never paid much attention to his classwork ... Gym ... How he would rub his "A's" in Physical Education into Geoffrey's face and mock his brother's merciful "C". Myles usually got his "C" in math, but a "D" in English. Yet one English class made an impact as he squirmed in anticipation of recess. On this day his teacher read a story by some writer from a hundred years ago named Edward Allen Joe or something or other. He recalled how terrified some guy was because he woke up in a coffin. But then he realized he was only sleeping in a cramped boat berth. *That's it!* Myles's spirits suddenly rose. '*I'm only having a nightmare. I'm actually sleeping in my bed -- even better-- my mommy's bed!*

* * *

"The Preston's invited me to their dinner party, so I can't very well ask Dolores to take my place ..."

"How about Betty Kirby?"

"Betty Kirby!" Lenore wound up with the phone like Tom Seaver pitching to Hank Aaron. Suddenly she remembered the mess she had to clean because Lance hurled a full beer bottle after an Eagles fumble. Her jittery hands placed the phone back on its table. "I wouldn't trust Betty Kirby to fill in for the cleaning woman, much less the Junior League auction."

* * *

Myles breathed through his nose and smelled his mother's sweet perfume. Expecting to see dawn shine through her window, he opened his eyes ... *Darkness!* Abruptly the stench of fear roiled his stomach. He still couldn't scream. Instinct told him that clanking his brain against his inner skull would bring merciful unconsciousness. "Bang! Bang! Bang!" The brat started smacking the back of his head into the closet wall.

* * *

"Obviously you have important societal commitments. I understand. Look. This spring I'm entering a solo race from the Bahamas to the Azores, so I really do need to brush up on my solo sailing skills. I'll call you in the new year. Maybe then we can ..."

Lenore fought her sphincter. "No! No! I've got a solution ..."

* * *

Hammering, hammering, hammering, like a drumbeat from one of his Uncle Check's rock albums, Myles's headbanging reverberated its way into Lenore's bedroom. She hastened her speech. "Helen Murchinson. She was quite peeved when Elizabeth Endicott picked me over her. Not only is Helen qualified, but yielding the Junior League auction to her will help smooth ruffled feathers. And seeing that I can trust you to act as a gentleman, what I think is, that I think I'll accept your offer."

"Well then pack your bags. I'll pick you up Friday. Oh, by the way... Myles. Will he be alright with you going away with me and not spending Christmas with him?"

"Bang! Bang! Bang!"

Lenore cupped the mouthpiece. "Well, at first, he might be a little disappointed at my going away over Christmas, but I'll have him stay with his grandparents. He'll have such a great time that he'll get over it in no time. Don't you worry about Myles. I have him well taken care of."

* * *

The first monster attacked stealthily. Just a tingling. Six tickling feet walked up his ankle, ending Myles's brain jarring jaunt into la-la-land. He slapped the invisible creeper.

* * *

Although the darkness muffled his howl, his tortured grunt harmonized with the sharp pain of the wasp sting. At last, he found the resolve to gain footing. He charged his tomb's door! His forehead struck the wooden door more surely than the back of his head ever did the plaster wall... Not aware of how long he had lost consciousness or when he regained it, he found himself seated in the corner again, hugging his knees. He sensed that the hot blood flow on his face and his leg's scorching sting boded the eternal damnation that awaited after the monsters killed him. *Helpless... Helpless... Helpless... Rescue me. Somebody rescue me!* "Mommy! Mommy!" he yelled. "Mommy!" The brat leapt up and pounded the door. "Mommy! Mommy! Mommy!" The door's percussion echoed about his blackened crypt. "Maw-Mee!" His tears sprinkled a shower of fear. At first, the searing brightness compounded his torment. Through the blinding effulgence, the marble-like face of his mother started to crystallize. "Mommy!" The brat recognized the image. He fell to his knees, bent over, hugged her ankles, and cried at her feet.

# Chapter 16

Excited as a well-prepared student about to read his exam results, Scotch Sutton loped into psychiatrist Eduardo Tryvye's office. The doctor had his face buried behind a folder. Scotch heard a faint rattling sound. He also detected that the psychiatrist's concealed hand was wiggling something behind the brief. "Dr. Tryvye. You said you had the results."

"Ya. Ya. Ya." Dr. Tryvye stuffed the folder with a hidden, clear plastic box into a drawer of his aircraft carrier-like desk. He winced on spotting a tiny steel pellet rolling out the clown's nose. The doctor hastily shuffled some other briefs.

"Well?" Scotch stood at the desk's edge.

"According to Marvin Smith, he's the examiner, Geoffrey exhibited no overt manifestations of external stress."

"You mean, Geoffrey told the truth. He passed!"

"I said he exhibited no overt manifestations of external stress. That's the extent of a polygraph result, Mr. Sutton. A Borderline Personality disorder is caused by the anxiety of the conscious mind denying the reality that the subconscious mind acknowledges."

"But he passed the test!"

"All that we can extrapolate from the polygraph results is that his conscious mind told the truth. Only his subconscious mind is cognizant of empirical reality. Extensive analysis is required to unearth the mysteries of his subconscious mind. Until I gain the analytical insight to help the boy gain a manifest understanding of his subconscious mind's hidden dynamics, a reconciliation with its recognition of reality, and a cessation of pathological denial, Geoffrey must stay with me."

"How long will that take?"

"Years, Mr. Sutton. Perhaps years and years."

# Chapter 17

Myles lay on his bed watching *Gilligan's Island* on T.V."

Lenore entered. "Come on Myles. It's time to go to Granddad and Grandma's."

"I told you! I told you! I told you! I ain't goin'! And I wanna watch this show. It's funny. They gotta chance to get off the island, but watch Gilligan." Myles pointed at the T.V. "I bet he fucks it up."

Lenore lurched forward. "You watch your mouth!" She prodded.

"Ya, well, I said, 'I bet'." He jutted his jaw. "So I wanna watch you put your *money* where *your mouth* is. A quarter says that's what's gonna happen."

"If you're so sure about what's going to happen, then you don't need to watch," Lenore switched off the T.V., "do you?"

"Hey. Tum that back on! Anyway, there's a whole bunch of cool cartoons comin' on next."

"You can watch them at the farm." Lenore prodded. "Let's go."

Myles stood and glared at his mother. "I said-- I ain't goin'!" Myles perused his mother. How lovely she looked in her knee-length beige skirt. It was topped by a double-breasted beige blouse fastened by brass buttons. He saw a vision of himself sucking milk from her nipples. And her perfume? *So sweet.* "How much are you charging him?"

"What on Earth are you talking about?"

"Wayne Madison? How much is he paying for sex?"

"Huhhh!" She slapped his face. "You're twelve years old!" Lenore prodded. "It's time you learn about the birds and the bees, and accept it."

Myles massaged his inflamed cheek. "Ya!" He shouted and sprayed tears. "I just hope you're chargin' Wayne Madison more than the bees get from the birds."

"You little ... Bastard!" Lenore clapped his other cheek.

"Fuck you!" Myles flipped her the finger. "Whore!"

For three pregnant seconds, mother and son squared off. Suddenly the brat's right fist punched her chin. He followed with a left hook to the side of her jaw.

Lenore fell onto her back.

Myles, arms flared at sides, stood over her. "You can kiss my ass if you think I'm gonna be a good little boy and let you hide me on the farm while you fuck Wayne for Christmas." He jutted his head.

The brat's grotesquely contorted face burned through Lenore's fog. Reflexively she kicked his testicles.

"Ughhhhh!" He clenched his privates, vainly attempting to contain the rupturous agony. His gut rose into his skull. Like electrons circling an atomic nucleus, his stomach and brain chased each other.

Lenore stood. "Clap!" She cuffed his face. "So that's the way you want it. Well, it's my Christmas too! Not only am I spending it with Wayne Madison, but you're going to accept it and like it. Now shut up and come with me to the farm -- Peacefully!"

His fury surged. Intense physical torment prevented thought. Only his aggravated stomach responded. The brat hurled on his mother's blouse.

"You spoiled, rotten, little...Shit! So you don't want to spend a week at the farm, huh? Fine with me." Lenore snatched Myles by the ear. "Instead you get to spend it in Geoffrey's retard closet!" She dragged him down the hallway. "You don't believe me? Remember how long he'd spend inside?" The mother pitched her younger son into the closet and locked the door. "Merry Christmas!"

Lenore spent the next hour rinsing her puke-soiled blouse, bathing her sullied body, and reapplying her makeup. She changed into a navy blue dress. Afterward, she opened the closet.

Myles sat in the corner. A dollop of feces provided a soft, warm seat. He was hugging his knees. His mind couldn't articulate *'want' 'need'*. "Waaaaa .... Waaaaa ... Waaaaa." he squalled.

"Oh," Lenore pinched her nose, "shit." She lifted him by the shirt scruff.

He allowed her to pull him into the bathroom. Lenore stumbled him into the bathtub, soon showering him with cold water. She stripped his pants and scrubbed his buttocks and upper thighs. The fetid mess mingled with soap suds, swirling down the drain. Next, she soaped his bruised genitals.

Gradually, he regained his senses. "Mommy! Mommy!" He cried. "Don't leave me! Please don't ever leave me!"

"I'm only going for a week, honey. Granddad and Grandma love you. You'll have lots of fun. I promise." Lenore turned off the shower and started toweling his naked body.

"Mommy." Myles hugged her.

She then led him by the hand to his bedroom. She helped him put on a dry pair of blue jeans and a green plaid, flannel shirt.

They experienced an uneventful drive in the new Buick Electra. Within twenty minutes, they approached the Amish-crested barn and white double-storied farmhouse. Scotch and Dolly Sutton stood outside waiting.

"Well, hello there Myles." Scotch opened the car door. Head down, Myles grunted: "Hi."

Lenore alighted unassisted. "You're going to have a great time with Granddad and Grandma. Aren't you?"

"Uh." Myles glanced back, curling his lip to her.

"Well, I've got something to cheer you up." Scotch pumped his fist. "I know it's not Christmas yet, but Mr. Madison dropped it off and told me to give it to you right away."

Dolly Sutton walked to the porch and returned with a gift-wrapped, oblong package. "Look at this, Myles. I don't know what's inside. But I bet it's something special."

The brat's eyes opened wide—abruptly, he stifled his grin. "Nah." He sneered and looked away. "I don't want it."

"Sure you do." Scotch put his arm around the boy's shoulder. "Here. We'll open it together." The grandfather unwrapped the gift. "Oh, well, look at this. I wish I had one when I was a boy."

Myles grabbed the present's brass barrel. He smiled.

"I'll tell Wayne that you said thank you," Lenore added.

Myles squeezed the Daisy air rifle's wooden stock and

imagined it as a real gun. His heart throbbed as he pictured blood spouting from Wayne's fresh bullet holes.

"I just knew you'd love it," Dolly added. "Come on inside. I baked you some fresh brownies. Say goodbye to your mother."

"Bye." He scowled and grunted. A moment later, he was stuffing his face with his grandmother's baked confection.

"Are you sure you're doing the right thing, leaving your son for Christmas?" Scotch asked.

"I know he doesn't seem too happy right now. But he'll get over it. Kids always do. After all, where better for a young boy than a farm? Furthermore, considering the trauma caused by recent events, a change of place can only do him a world of good. Keeping that in mind, please father, rather you don't even mention Geoffrey. Make this a time of recovery for Myles."

"Are you sure that's the right thing? What if Geoffrey is innocent? Wouldn't you then want them to ..."

"Please Father." Lenore held up a policeman's stiff arm. "When the time is right. For now, let this be a week of healing." She checked her watch. "Sorry father. I really got to go. I was unexpectedly held up for an hour."

* * *

"Lenore Burkett." She placed her elbows on the private airport's information counter and leaned toward the receptionist. "Lawrence Wainwright Madison III is expecting me."

"Yes, Ma'am." Both names alerted the eighteen-year-old receptionist. She promptly clicked a switchboard lever and spoke into a microphone. The blue and white uniformed girl flashed teeth with braces. "Wait right here. Someone will be with you in seconds."

"Afternoon, Ma'am!" A black uniformed, broad-bill-hatted chauffeur grabbed Lenore's single suitcase. "Come right this way, Ma'am!"

"Right what way?" Lenore shrugged.

"This way, Ma'am." He opened the limousine's rear door. "You do want to meet Mr. Madison at his plane, don't you, Ma'am?" Lenore climbed into the car.

After three minutes of weaving between Pipers, Beachcraft, and Leers, the Black Lincoln limousine stopped in front of a dual-prop Cessna 402. Wayne Madison, foot boosted on air stairs, forearm on knee, awaited. The chauffeur alighted and approached the gentleman. He briefed the driver, then tipped him.

"Why... Thank you, thank you very much." He grinned at Andrew Jackson's tactiturn portrait. "Anything else I can do for you,

Mr. Madison?"

Wayne shook his head.

After tipping his cap, the driver ambled over and opened Lenore's door.

She alighted. She opened her eyes wide and arched her eyebrows. "Does this plane belong to you?" Her voice rose a pitch.

"Yep." Wayne slapped the fuselage. The white, green-blazed Cessna 402 resembled a pelagic shark with colossal pectoral fins. "She's all mine and she's ready to soar." Wayne heaved Lenore's suitcase through the open hatch, then extended his hand. "Come. We have a lot of flying ahead of us." Wayne clenched her clammy hand and hiked her into the cockpit. She sat crash test dummy still. After leaning over and buckling her in, he spoke into his headset's mouthpiece. "Cessna 58209, preparing to taxi from tarmac." After two lever clicks and a button push, the dual engines came to life. The plane then began a five-minute taxi. "We're at the final approach. Last chance to turn around." Without waiting for Lenore's reply, Wayne spoke into the radio. "Cessna 58209 to traffic. Waiting for the all-clear at runway five."

"Traffic to Cessna 58209. You have the all-clear for runway five."

"Thank you. Over and out." After performing the run-up,

Wayne raced his plane down the runway like a hot-rodder behind the wheel of a Deuce Coupe.

The G-force pegged Lenore into the backrest. She gritted her teeth and clamped the armrest. "Nervous?" Wayne asked.

"No, no." Lenore's orbs twirled in their sockets. "First Flight?"

Lift-off!

''No, no. Of course not." She watched the panorama reduce from model railroad 0-scale, to S-scale, to HO-scale, to N-scale. That aspect of her first flight was only a secondary concern... She recalled hers and Lance's honeymoon. He drove her to the Nation's Capital-- ten days after their wedding. Why did he insist on waiting so long after the wedding? Her sitting with him in the grandstand of Washington D.C.'s Griffith's field, watching the Redskins battle the Eagles, answered that question.

"We've reached the North-East bay." Wayne pointed out the window. "I'm going to drop altitude and follow the Intracoastal Waterway along the Chesapeake Bay, right out to the Atlantic Ocean."

"The scenery is overwhelming," she answered. "Such wide, blue water... The little islands, huge bluffs, and twisting rivers."

"As pristine as this natural beauty looks, we're, believe it or not, flying over the hemisphere's busiest shipping lane. It starts due east with the Chesapeake-Delaware Canal, which links the bay to Philadelphia, the world's largest freshwater port. About forty miles south, and we'll reach the headwaters to Baltimore. Next is the Naval Academy at Annapolis. The route veers to the open sea at Norfolk, Virginia."

"Wow. You sound like an expert travel guide."

Wayne chuckled. "Sorry I can't describe it in more personal terms. Well, anyway, this part of the country is among my personal favorites. Believe it or not, you'll soon see, that much of the coast consists of private farms or forest, so it's inaccessible by car. That leaves only two ways to experience it. By boat or air. Three years ago, I won the Philadelphia to Norfolk solo sailing race. It took me five days. You're going to see the whole thing in about the time it takes to watch a movie."

"Are you happy not to fly it solo?"

Wayne grinned and squeezed Lenore's hand.

* * *

Myles, air rifle in hand, stalked about the farm, imagining himself in Africa hunting big game. He hid behind a tree and aimed at a squirrel. "Pop," sounded the air gun. "Shit," said the brat as the pellet ricocheted against bare branches, missing the rodent. He then stole into the barn-- the panther's lair! Myles spotted the beast's owlish eyes and dropped to his belly. Bravely he pointed his gun. The man-eating predator was poised to attack from a roof beam. "Pop!"

Rowww!" shrieked Sasha the cat as the steel pellet struck her ribs. "Pop! Pop!" Myles blasted away at the cat. Sasha swiftly scuttled to the safety of the loft.

Alarmed by his pet's agonized screech, Norman hopped into the barn. A cannibal attack! Myles turned his gun on the old man.

"Hey, what do you think you're doing?" Norman leaned on his crutch and raised his palms. "Trying to hurt my Sasha? You are one horrible little boy, do you know that?"

"Nigger, nigger, stop your snigger, or I'm gonna pull this trigger."

"You will do no such thing. You give me that." Norman hopped forward. "I'll give it to your grandfather. He'll decide if and when you get it back."

"Ooga booga! Ooga booga!" The brat shot the old man's forehead.

Norman felt a metallic sting, a concussive thud, and saw a fiery flash. He fell on his back, the rear of his head striking the barn's wooden floor ... The recent runaway faced a tusk-mustached sheriff,

"If there's one thing I hate more than a dirty nigger boy," the lawman with arms like wagon spokes clutched the teenager by the hair. "It's a dirty, crippled nigger boy. There," the three hundred and fifty-pounder pushed the barrel of his .44 magnum into Norman's nose. ''Now your nose is even flatter." *'Click.'* He cocked the hammer. "But boy, all's I gotta do is pull this here trigger, and your nose gits spread all the way to the Mason-Dixon line. So what ya best do, boy, is start hoppin', and don't look back till ya git outta my county." Norman opened his eyes and saw a leering brat straddling him. He pumped the BB gun's cocking mechanism and pointed the barrel between his eyes. "Ooga Booga. Ooga Booga. Get up. Cannibal!"

Norman used his hands to slide his body back a yard. Painfully he climbed to his good foot. "Hop, nigger! Hop!" Myles jabbed him with the gun barrel.

The old man had no choice but to hop out of the barn, steel pellet sparks spurring him. He dared not look back, even after staggering into the guest house. A chest tightening dropped Norman to the floor. He clutched his thorax and panted. Although the rules had changed since he ran away during the depression, old lessons are hard forgotten. Scotch would never hear of the incident.

"Ha! Ha! Ha! Ha! Ha! Ha!" Myles guffawed.

"Meowww!" Sasha, coiled to strike, hissed and growled from a roof beam.

"Huh." The brat raised his gun. Before he could pull the trigger, the enraged feline was on his face. "Mowww! Reowww!" She gashed his cheeks before he could react. He swatted at air. The cat now clawed his chest. Myles dropped his gun and ran. Sasha sprang and tore a forget-me-not into his buttocks before he escaped.

* * *

"Look below." Wayne pointed. "The Chesapeake Bay Bridge-Tunnel. At 17.6 Miles, she's the longest of her kind in the world. She cost $200,000,000-00 to build. Do you know how much of that your tax dollars contributed?"

"All of it?" Lenore shrugged.

"Not a dime. Every penny came from private funds. I own a share of it. So I have a vested interest in each of those little cars and trucks you see driving across. For me she's the boom gate to the Atlantic Ocean." Wayne turned to Lenore. "Nice dress."

"Thank you." Lenore clutched her collar and perused her jacket. "Sergio, Elizabeth Endicott's new designer, made it for me."

"I surely won't challenge Sergio's style mandate for Pennsylvania in December. But we're headed for the tropics. So I'm going to radio Bermuda and talk to a Mr. DePlume. You may remember him as Stanforth's most pouplar beautician. I guess some people in Stanforth weren't ready for him."

"I remember him. He was my Mother's favorite. Then some juvenile delinquent named Bucky Butz beat the hell out of him just because he was," Lenore sctatched her head, "Um, gay,"

"Well times have changed."

"Yeah, it seems no one minds that Marion Endicott is . . ."

"Shh…" Wayne put his finger in front of his lips. "We aren't supposed to talk about that. Well, anyway, Mr DePlume has moved up to be the tropical fashion king." Wayne then spoke French into the radio. Sharply he banked the plane to the southeast.

"Hey!" Only Lenore's seat belt stopped her from tumbling into the pilot. "What are you doing?"

"'I'm changing course. We're now headed for Bermuda."

"Bermuda? Sounds exciting. But what ever for?"

"You do want Mr. DePlume to measure you up for a new tropical wardrobe? Don't you?"

"Why yes. Yes of course." Lenore beamed.

* * *

The next morning, Myles resumed his hunt. This time, he

was more than a sportsman. Now, his search-and-destroy mission possessed him with jihad fervor. "The nigger's cat's gonna pay. I'm going to kill her nine times over just to be certain," Myles said aloud as he squeezed his rifle's stock. Earlier, he told his grandfather that he got his scratches by slipping on the gravel driveway. *'Mommy, before he arrived anyway, would've taken one look at my cuts and had the demon cat killed without question,'* Myles thought. *'Granddad always asks too many questions. Sometimes he even sided with Geoffrey. I bet he likes him as much as the nigger does. Knowing granddad, he might even side against me with the nigger and his devil cat. I bet he even likes the crippled old shit more than he likes me.'* "This time it's just you and me buddy," Myles said to his air rifle. "They're gonna pay. They're all gonna pay."

"Myles!" Scotch shouted.

*'What does he want?'* Myles ignored him.

"Myles!" Scotch ran up to the brat.

"Yeah?" Myles turned.

"How would you like to enjoy a chicken feast tonight?" The brat moistened his lips.

"But first," Scotch continued. "You gotta help me pick out the oldest and fattest rooster on the farm."

"Are you gonna kill him?"

"Yes. But the rooster will understand."

"Huh?"

"You see Myles, God made some creatures herbivores. That's a plant eater. Others he made carnivores. That's a meat eater. Man is what's called an omnivore. That means, unless we're very careful, we need to eat both plants and meat to stay healthy. I'll show you the teeth of Miss Kaye the cow. All of her teeth are like our rear teeth. That's because all she eats are plants, which her molars grind down. If you look at a meat eater like Chester A. Dawg or one of Norman's cats, you'll see that all their teeth are like our front teeth. That's because they need to hold and slash meat. Now you know why we have both kinds of teeth. Also, a carnivore has a far shorter digestive tract than a herbivore. Ours is somewhere in between..."

"You sound like one of my teachers."

"Then you'll be all set and get a good grade. What I bet they won't teach you in school is that man has a unique contract with the animal kingdom. Unfortunately, man often breaks that contract."

"I don't understand." Myles scratched his head.

"Nature is God's art. Even the most simple of man's art is an arrangement of parts. Each part depends on the other to make a perfect whole. God's art is the same. Herbivores gain life by absorbing the life of the plants. The meat eating animals do the same by consuming the plant-eating animals. Then when the carnivores die, they, in turn, return to the soil, feeding the plants. Think of it as the circle of life. Yes, God gave us dominion over the animals, but he also charges us with a great responsibility to take care of our natural environment."

"Now I understand." Myles pointed his air rifle at a rooster. "Can I shoot that big fat one?"

"Oh no Myles. If you don't score a perfect hit, that rooster may suffer. Part of our bargain with the animal kingdom is that when the end comes, we do it as quickly and painlessly as possible. We, as higher beings, owe that to the rooster. A wolf or fox would tear him apart. Let's respect nature and do what we have to do as humanely as possible."

Scotch and Myles walked into the barn.

"How are we supposed to kill him so much better than a wolf would?"

"With this." Scotch picked up a hatchet

Myles grinned. His pupils dilated wildly.

Scotch soon performed the macabre necessity. The drop-jawed grandfather shivered as the brat guffawed at the decapitated chicken's aimless death run.

* * *

Wayne and Lenore walked hand in hand on the docks of Puerto Rico's Ponce DeLeon harbor. Her new silk and cotton, lavender floral sun dress fluttered with the gentle, warm breeze. She pinched the broad brim of her white sun hat, securing it against the trade wind. The Caribbean coast executive marina bedazzled her as much as the private airport. A hundred and thirty-foot long range cruiser with a helicopter parked atop the deck! An ninety-foot triple mast clipper! Each ambassadorial yacht heightened her anticipation of Wayne's boat and her cruise to never ending paradise?

"There she is." Wayne pointed.

"That's *your* boat." Lenore's face dropped like a privileged teenager expecting a birthday gift of a Harley-Davidson motorcycle but getting a Schwinn safety bicycle instead. That Wayne's skiff was dubbed "Dorothy" added training wheels.

"She sure is! I had her custom made." Wayne stepped onto the nineteen-foot skiff's gunnel and lowered Lenore's suitcase onto the stem deck. "I designed her fin-keel hull for maximum hydrodynamics and her low, wedge-shaped cabin for maximum aerodynamics. She's only six feet across at her widest. That's so she can cut through the waves like a hot knife through butter. She's got all that we need: a sextant, compass, and charts. I'll rig her a broad-seam sail and a spinnaker, and we'll ride the trade winds to the Phosphorous bay almost as fast as a motorboat!"

"But. But."

Wayne noticed her forlorn expression. "Hey, look, we don't have to go sailing. I can always check us into a five-star hotel, separate rooms, if you prefer."

"It's just that I . . ."

"It's just that you expected a Lawrence Wainwright Madison III to own a pompous floating status symbol, something to prove to the world just how much money the Madisons are worth? Didn't you?"

"No. No." Lenore guarded mouth with hand. "Um, well, It's just that when, well, um, when you said a racing skiff, I pictured a yacht like on the cover of *Sports Illustrated* "

"You mean the America's Cup?"

"Yes." Lenore's arms covered her breasts.

"I once owned a class II racing yacht. But do you know how many crew members an America's Cup yacht requires? Sure. Francis Bacon said, 'Whosoever is delighted in solitude is either a wild beast or a God.' Well, I assure you that I'm neither of the above. But Lenore, out there," Wayne pointed toward the horizon, "the sea becomes your friend, companion, and even lover. The psalmists tell us 'they that go down to the sea in ships, that do business in great waters; these see the works of the Lord, and his wonders in the deep.' I thought you would want to experience that just with me, without the proverbial maddening crowd. Dorothy helped build my little baby." Wayne slapped his racing skiff's hull. "If you don't even want to sail in it, I'll understand." Wayne, hands in a fist, crossed his arms.

Lenore scanned the harbor like a rodent surveying a Skinner box. She leapt onto the stem deck. "Such a lovely breeze!" She wrapped her arm around Wayne's waist. "We better cast off while she still blows."

Wayne slipped from her embrace. He pinched his chin. A moment later he unwound the boat's tether rope from the harbor cleat. After puttering his skiff out of the harbor under auxiliary, Wayne announced, "We've got a fifteen-knot wind and glassy seas. It won't get any better than this. The Dorothy may not be the Queen Mary, but she isn't a Spartan slave barge either. I've wired it with a stereo sound system. Wayne clicked a button. Wagner's 'Flying Dutchman Overture' blasted from speakers tactically installed about the boat. He reappeared with a bright orange nylon bag and tossed it atop the cabin deck. "Let's set sail." He climbed onto the cabin deck. "Come on. Help me." He boosted her by the hand. They then ran the white and green broad-beamed sail up the mast. "I'll cast the spinnaker. You take the helm."

"Huh?" Lenore nibbled on her knuckles. "The wheel! Take the wheel."

"But I don't ... What shall I do?"

"Steer her leeward!"

"What?" Lenore shrieked and shrugged her shoulders.

"All you gotta do is get behind the wheel and drive her as you would a car." Lenore stumbled into the transom and grasped the helm.

"*Now t*urn her leeward."

"What?"

"The wind! Steer her with the wind!"

Lenore anxiously wheeled the boat to two o'clock. Wayne cast the emerald-green spinnaker. "Look out!" He leapt from the cabin deck and pushed Lenore's head down. The boom sliced inches above, fluffing her hair.

"Wayne! I could have been killed!"

"Nonsense!" Wayne wrapped his left arm across her chest and grabbed the wheel with his right hand. "You would've just gotten a little headache."

"A little headache?" Lenore looked forward. She saw only cobalt ocean and endless horizon. A spray of frothy salt stung her eyes. Again and again, the skiff cut through the waves. Lenore buried her eyes into Wayne's chest. "Land? I can't see land! We're lost at sea."

"If you'd look to the starboard, you'll see some of the world's most idyllic beaches." Lenore looked to her left. "Water! I can only see water!"

"That's because you're looking to the port. The starboard's that way." Wayne turned Lenore's head.

"Okay. Okay. I see land. But it looks miles away."

"Really? I could've swum us there when I was younger."

"When you were younger? A lot of good that would do us now!"

"Why worry? We'd never drown."

"You sound sure of yourself."

"Of course. The sharks would eat us long before we'd have to worry about drowning."

"Wayne!" Lenore covered her eyes. "Take me back. Take me back!" She shook her arms. "Please! I'm not meant for this sea adventure stuff."

"We're hardly out on an adventure. This is just a tour."

"Yeah. And that's all Gilligan and the skipper took their party out for."

"Here." Wayne grabbed a rope. "I'll secure the boom to the runners." Wayne looped the line figure eight over the port cleat. "Relax." He pressed Lenore close to him. "Enjoy the ride. We're only an hour of smooth sailing from Phosphorous Bay."

Lenore snuggled her back into Wayne's chest. His arms squeezed her python tight. Ten gasps later, she felt secure. A 107-foot luxury cruiser tooted. The dapper captain tipped his naval hat and waved to them...

* * *

Luxuriant Palm trees dotted the shore of the Phosphorus bay. The fragrance of tropical flowers, bananas, mangoes, and coconuts spiced the salty air. A beach with sand fluffy and white as mineralized rocky mountain snow awaited just a relaxing swim away. "Lap, lap," the still waters caressed The Dorothy's hull. Wayne and Lenore lay upon a soft cushion cast atop the bow deck. "To you, my Senta." Wayne tapped his crystal goblet of Dom Perignon to Lenore's.

"Thank you, my Dutchman, for safeguarding me through the

wild and stormy sea." That toast to characters from the *Flying Dutchman* opera despite Act II of *Tristan and Isolde* playing from the stereo. Lenore and Wayne locked arms. Together they sipped Champaign.

"Ah, such a beautiful full moon." Wayne put his arm around Lenore's shoulder. "Did you know that a different moon shines over the Caribbean?"

"No?"

Wayne chuckled.

"All right, hey," Lenore chuckled, "I hope you don't think I didn't catch your little quip. But I must say," she lay back, using Wayne's arm as a pillow, "the moon here does seem larger and brighter than the one over Cape May."

"Roll over to your side and you'll see a sight unique only to this little nook of the planet."

"Huh? My God! The water…"

"I assure you that you're not seeing things." Wayne turned to his side, facing Lenore. "The water really is glowing."

"But how? Am I witnessing a miracle?"

"Sort of. Call it one of nature's miracles. The Phosphorus Bay got its namesake owing to microscopic phosphorus deposits in the water. On clear, full moon evenings such as this, the phosphorus does indeed cause the water to glow.”

“Thank you, Wayne. Without you, could I ever experience this?” Lenore pecked his lips. In less than a second, Wayne transformed Lenore’s peck into a sustained lip lock. Lap, lap, lub, dub sounded the bay buffeting the hull. Their tongues linked, sealing the kiss. Switching his fluttering passion to her earlobes, his hands buffed her back. “Rip,” went the Velcro binding of her Mr. DePlume-designed bikini top. After kissing her neck, his chin pushed aside the loosened bikini top. Lenore panted to the beat of the lapping waters as his lips ringed her nipples. His tongue flickers made her moan in harmony with the tropical breeze. She clawed the back of his neck as his kisses slid down her abdomen. Wayne’s fingertips stimulated an electrolyte sensation down her bare hips as her bikini bottom fell by the wayside. Within moments, she was clamping his ears like a cliff purchase, her screams punctuating each climax. Five minutes later, his nibbling mouth climbed back up her stomach. He gave her navel an extra five-seconds. Soon her jack-knifed knees squeezed his outer thighs. A hard rubber-like spike rubbed her inner thighs.

“Wait, wait,” she said. Lap, lap, lub, dub, the bay continued to buffet the boat.

“Can’t wait; why wait?”

"No, no. Not yet."

"Not yet? Why not?"

"Betty Kirby."

"Betty Kirby?"

"Betty Kirby. Talk to Elizabeth Endicott. Have her remove Betty Kirby from the committee."

"We can't, now, talk about…"

"She called Elizabeth Endicott crazy; didn't she? That won't help the committee; will it?" Lap, lap, lub, dub, the bay cuffed the boat.

*Tap Tap*, his penis at her entrance.

"Wayne." Her eyes crossed.

"Okay. Okay. I'll do it." Stroking. Stroking. Stroking. His erection moved like a chisel sculpting an erotic masterpiece.

* * *

Dolly Sutton awoke with a fright. "Scotch, I hear something."

"I'm sure it's just the wind." Scotch pulled the blankets over his head. "Go back to sleep."

"No. There. Did you hear that? The barn."

"I'm sure it's nothing Norman can't handle," Scotch grumbled. "I'm worried that we have intruders."

This time Scotch heard the muffled chaos of clanging tools, banging wooden planks, a dog howling, cats panicking, and frenzied chickens. "You're right, Dolly. Now I do hear something." A pajama-clad Scotch climbed out of bed and snatched a winter coat from the closet. "I better check it out." He pulled on a pair of boots.

"No. Please, dear. Rather just call the police."

"Don't worry. I'll be careful. I better make sure it is a burglar, and not just a wild animal. I don't want to call the police on a false alarm."

Scotch, unarmed, inched along his barn's outside wall. He turned a corner. Norman was leaning against the barn. His crutch and cane lay crossed at his feet like a soldier's surrendered arms. The new foreman's lips stuttered before he murmured. "I'm sorry, I. I. Couldn't stop him."

Scotch put his forefinger before his lips. "Shh," he held up the halt gesture. Pressing his right hand against his chest, Scotch vainly attempted to silence his heartbeat. Next, he heard laughter. Scotch sighed and walked into the barn. For two full seconds, the grandfather's heart stopped. Someday in the future, blood and carnage will cover the Valley of Armageddon to a depth of a horse's bridle. The gory puddles scattered about the barn made an apocalyptic preview. Myles, bloody hatchet in hand, guffawed. He had decapitated all of the chickens.

* * *

"Mommy!" Myles ran from the Suttons' front porch and hugged his mother after she exited her Buick.

"Awww ... I'm happy to see you too, honey." She returned the hug and patted his back. "Were Grandfather and Grandmother nice to you?"

"Yes, Mommy. But I'm glad I'm going home. I missed you, Mommy."

"Well, I missed you too, honey!" Lenore looked to her parents. "And was Myles a good boy?" She immediately noticed their peculiar expressions.

"Come, Myles," Dolly said. "Don't you want to say goodbye to Chester A. Dawg?"

"No. I wanna stay with mommy."

Scotch sharpened his gaze.

"You go with Grandma." Lenore gently pushed Myles away. "Play with the dog. We'll go home in a minute."

"No! He's going to lie about me!" The brat, resolutely maintained his embraceand pointed at Scotch.

Dolly tugged on Myles's coat sleeve. The brat released his

maternal hug and squared his feet at his grandmother.

Lenore walked up to her father and asked in a muffled growl: "What's the problem?"

Scotch turned his face away from Myles. "Lenore, I don't want to upset you, but something alarming happened."

"What?" Lenore placed hands on her hips.

Scotch glanced at his wife trying to restrain Myles. "Rather, we don't talk about it here. Let's call Eduardo Tryvye. He's very intimate with the trauma our family has faced. I think a brief session with Myles would do us all wonders."

"Dr. Tryvye?" Lenore spoke with a minimal of lip movement. "Look. We have only one nut in this family and that's Geoffrey. His shrink isn't far behind. My baby's got enough adversity to face without you spouting accusations. After all, his brother murdered his father. Now he sees me with a new man. I think that's enough for him to cope with, don't you?" Lenore prodded. "The last thing he needs is you upsetting him. So whatever it is you don't like about my baby, it's a phase." Lenore turned and walked toward Myles. "He's going through a phase and nothing more." She took her brat by the hand and walked him to the Buick.

Myles stuck his tongue out at Scotch before getting into the car.

# Chapter 18

"Well, there she is! What do ya think?" Scotch Sutton, standing on the Lancaster, Pennsylvania, train station's main platform, pointed to the K4 Pacific 4-6-4 steam locomotive. During the nineteenth century, the public often called steam engines iron horses. This early 20th-century successor more resembled an African river horse. A hippopotamus. The stout engine was black as the coal that fueled her. Her smokestack rose sixteen feet above seven mist and vapor hissing, piston-driven wheels. She spanned fifty feet from front to rear bogie.

"Wow! And we get to ride behind her all the way to Philadelphia!" For his first furlough from Harlond State Mental Hospital, Geoffrey accompanied psychiatrist Eduardo Tryvye and orderly Victor Washington. Norman also joined them for this special event. An exhibition steam train run.

"No." Scotch eyed the seven Tuscan red, early 20th-century passenger coaches. "You don't get to ride behind her."

"What?" Geoffrey whined. "But you promised." He dangled his arms at his side. "That's okay I guess. Grand-dad. You'll never know how amazing I feel, just getting out of that place, even if only for today. So thank you anyway. Thank you."

"Well, you let that faith of yours keep that amazin' feelin', cause I sure have faith in you. You didn't do it. Soon everyone will know it, and you'll get out of there for good. I just gotta feelin' Jesus is gonna work ya a miracle." Scotch clapped his hands. "Miracles can happen you know-- look at the Mets-- and now look at yourself. You came here only expecting a ride in a passenger car. Well, guess what?" He grinned like a card player about to show his royal flush. "You get to ride up front-- in the engine cab!"

"Really?"

"Yes. Really."

"Awww right!" Geoffrey jumped up and down. "Well, all right!" Scotch pumped his fist.

"All aboard!" The engineer beckoned from the cab. Norman, who had already embarked, also waved.

"Let's not keep the engineer waiting. You go with Mr. Washington. I'll see you in Philadelphia."

The tall, muscular Black orderly scowled before walking two paces behind Geoffrey, en route to the train. The escort screened both the boy's body and shadow.

"Dr. Tryvye." Scotch pointed at Victor Washington's railroad track-wide back. "Is he really necessary?"

"Ya. Ya. Please understand, patients whose psychopathy has manifested in criminal behavior are almost never granted furloughs. As it is, he is still undergoing intense psychotherapy subsequent to patricide."

Scotch grimaced.

"Suspected patricide."

"Better." Scotch nodded.

"Regardless, today's outing manifestly diverges from procedure. So appreciate the magnitude of my magnanimity."

"That I most surely do." Scotch placed his hand on the psychiatrist's shoulder. "Nevertheless, he's a skinny thirteen-year-old boy. I could easily watch over him. Did you really need to bring someone who looks like he can block for the Eagles' quarterback?"

"I assure you that Mr. Washington executes his duties with utmost professionalism. Manifold are my obligations to both the patient and community. If I'm going to break procedure by allowing the boy a furlough, you must understand my need to exercise optimum precaution. Victor Washington," Dr. Tryvye pointed upward, "is the man most capable of executing that requirement."

"As well as a fine doctor, you're a great salesman." Scotch extended his right hand.

"Thank you for all you've done for my grandson. I'll see you in Philadelphia."

Dr. Tryvye smiled, shook Scotch's hand, then boarded the locomotive.

* * *

The steam train chugged across Lancaster County's farmland like an elephant stampeding over the African Savannah. Geoff Burkett could only watch the scenery through the front and port windows. Victor Washington stood in the starboard hatch, brawny arm braced across the threshold.

"What do you think of this baby?" Engineer Wendell Wright eyed a gauge, then adjusted the throttle accordingly.

"Wow!" Geoff beamed. "Its power! I can feel it in my feet."

"Powerful she is." The sixty-year-old engineer tipped his pinstriped, blunt-billed cap. "Her working pressure is a full 250 pounds per square inch." He wiped a bead of sweat and coal dust from his brow with a red bandanna. "She's got two cylinders. Each is 27 inches in diameter, with a 30-inch stroke. So you said it, young man, you are standing in one mighty piece of machinery."

"But she don't seem like a machine," Geoff said. "I feel like I'm in the brain of a giant, huffing and puffing beast."

"I'm afraid I'm the only brain she's got left, and those of us who know how to operate her are also dinosaurs."

"Maybe she's the behemoth of Job." Norman, seated next to the engineer, chuckled. "Behemoth is the word." Wendell downshifted the throttle and applied slight pressure to the brake. "She weighs 382,400 pounds; add 217,900 for the tender, and you got an over half-million pound beast-of-burden."

"Beast-of-burden?" Norman smiled at the engineer. "Seems to me like she's enjoyin' her work."

"Maybe that's because she knows she's headed home. She was born in Philadelphia, at the old Baldwin Locomotive Works."

"Ya." Norman pointed upward. "I know about the Baldwin Engineer Works. It was right near Shibe Park and the Baker Bowl."

"Baldwin Locomotive Works!" Victor Washington dropped his hands to hips and scowled. "My grandfather sweated his life away in that Hellhole. Twelve hours a day in the foundry. Do ya wanna know how little they paid him?"

Astonished, Wendell Wright turned to the orderly. "Do you mean to tell me that your grandfather had a hand in creating this magnificent machine?" The engineer extended his hand. "I'm honored to meet you, sir."

Victor Washington reluctantly shook the engineer's hand.

"As magnificent a machine as she is," the fireman beckoned Wendell and Victor away from the open boiler hatch, "she can't run on talk."

"My fireman's right. This Pacific's got more than 6,000 square feet of hungry boiler to feed. Here," Wendell took the fireman's shovel and handed it toward Victor. "Do you wanna feed her some coal?"

The orderly hunched his back, jutted his jaw, and clenched his fists.

"I want to!" Dr. Tryvye flapped his hands. "I want to. Let me. Let me!" The psychiatrist snatched the shovel and pitched coal into the boiler.

Norman beamed and laughed.

"Geoffrey. Let's give her more speed." Wendell took the boy's wrist and guided his hand to the brake. "Release her a click. Now take the throttle."

"Me?"

"Yes. You. Just squeeze the lever and move her up a notch." Geoffrey nervously complied.

"That's it, Geoff! Feel her going faster?"

"Ya! Ya!" The boy quaked. Norman continued his joyful

laughter.

"Look at all the people waving to us. Toot the whistle for them, Victor!"

"What?" Victor pulled his face.

"Toot the whistle! Here. Pull the chain."

The orderly shrugged and opened his hands. He strode over and half-pulled the chain. "Toot." Sounded the train.

"Come on!" The engineer urged him. "Pull the chain!"

"Toot! Toot!" Victor twice again yanked the whistle chain. "Toot! Toot!" This time Victor beamed wide as Broadway. "Toot! Toot!" He waved to the trackside spectators.

Norman now laughed jollier than Santa Claus on Christmas eve.

In about the time it took Wayne Madison to fly his Plane over the Chesapeake Bay's length, the train barreled past Paoli, the first town of Philadelphia's exclusive Main Line suburbs. After passing Stanforth Pennsylvania's train station, Norman looked out the port window to the clearing that once was his thicket shielded shack. He tightened his lips. Then he looked up the tracks and smiled. A moment later he tooted the whistle and waved to the spectators on the Stanforth station platform.

* * *

Philadelphia's Thirtieth Street Train Station covers a full city block. Its column and pilaster-laden, Greek temple facade hailed to a better era of public building style, before the plague of the modern factory aesthetic. Its Alabama limestone main waiting room impressed as a giant cavern. Chandeliers hung from its seven-storey-high ceiling like giant, illuminated stalactites. Scotch waited in the east end, under a 70-foot-high statue of Michael the Archangel. Entitled *'Angel of Resurrection'* Walter Hancock sculpted it as a World War II memorial. "So, did you have fun?" He asked Geoffrey.

"We had a wonderful time." Dr. Tryvye stepped forward. "Splendid! Magnificent!"

Scotch chuckled and refocused his gaze toward his grandson. "And you, Geoffrey?"

"Grand-dad. Why is everyone being so nice to me? Today was the funnest day of my life."

Scotch gently cuffed Geoffrey's shoulder. "Why shouldn't people be nice to you? You're a fine young man. You got a tough break and you've handled it like a man. A brave man." He turned slyly to the psychiatrist. "Isn't that right, Dr. Tryvye?"

"Ya. Ya. Ya." The doctor twitched his head parrot-like. "But I still don't want to go back to that place." Geoff plaintively looked at both his grandfather and psychiatrist.

"Of course, you don't. But you keep that courage and faith. You'll be coming home soon. "Soon, Geoff, soon." Scotch, hugging the boy, looked imploringly at Dr. Tryvye.

"I think the doc wants to rap with your Grandpop." Victor put his hand on Geoffrey's shoulder. "What do you say we cruise on over there," the orderly pointed eastward, "and get us some ice cream?"

"Yeah! Thanks!"

"And what's your flavor, Mr. Norman Bell?" Victor asked.

"Strawberry."

"Well, they got us 41 flavors. So I betcha they got ya at least five different kinds'a strawberry. Come on, everybody, it's on me." Victor nodded toward the ice cream stand.

"Bring me back one." Dr. Tryvye flapped his hands. "I wanna ice-cream too!"

* * *

Scotch looked toward Geoff, Victor, and Norman walking to the ice cream stand. "Dr. Tryvye, how can you still possibly believe that Geoff could've murdered his father?"

"Ah, ah, ah, Mr. Sutton." The psychiatrist, now sure that his orderly would bring him back an ice-cream cone, turned to the grandfather. "What did we discuss before? The neurotic patient's first mechanism of defense is to banish unpleasant memories from his consciousness and thus make them inaccessible. This mechanism, as I've explained before, is called repression. Repression creates a mental conflict. When that occurs, the emotion or memory that the patient wishes to make conscious and discharge, conflicts with the part of the mind which refuses to acknowledge or admit to, that same repellent effect. In Geoffrey's case, his superego has convinced his conscious mind of the odiousness of patricide; therefore, he has buried all memory of this repugnant act deep into his subconscious mind-- deep enough to have abandoned all memory of the event. Having achieved this consummate act of denial, he can now live what appears as a normal life. Unfortunately," Dr. Tryvye pointed upward, "the reality of the act and the internal turmoil that caused him to commit the nefarious deed in the first place remain. External stimulus or even internal spontaneity can cause an abreaction. If induced by extreme stress, a possible manifestation is a deadly fulmination. So you do understand why your grandson must remain under vigilant custody?"

"If it is true that he did ax his father, I would agree. Nevertheless, doctor, did you ever consider that the boy is indeed telling the truth, and never killed his father? Lance Burkett often acted in an impetuous and selfish manner, a sure formula for making enemies. I know all about the physical evidence against Geoffrey, but doesn't the possibility of the true perp framing the boy exist?"

Dr. Tryvye looked downward and scratched his head. "Yes, Mr. Sutton, I am starting to have my doubts."

"Your doubts?"

"Yes." The psychiatrist raised his head. "My doubts." He ruffled his hair. "I myself am starting to believe in the boy's innocence."

"I just wish I could find a way," Scotch shook his fist, "to prove it to you."

"Hmm," Dr. Tryvye pinched his chin. "Ahh," he pointed upward. "I do know a way."

"You do?" Scotch's face froze with hopeful anticipation.

"A method of enabling patients to recall the forgotten origins of particular symptoms does exist."

"Well, what is it Doctor?"

"Hypnosis."

"Hypnosis?"

"Yes, hypnosis. If I can successfully hypnotize the boy, and if he does recall, in sufficient detail, the events of the fateful afternoon of his father's murder, and if that recollection excludes his committing the homicide, then, I will release him into your care on an out-patient basis."

Scotch beamed. His smile crumbled like grains of sea sand creeping through clenched knuckles.

"Hmmm," Dr. Tryvye pinched his chin. "Ahhh," he pointed upward. "I sense a wave of melancholia washing over your consciousness. A long and arduous struggle finally crowned with success usually effects a state of joy, exultation, or triumph. Exonerating your grandson has given you an estimable, all-consuming purpose." The psychiatrist prodded. "Correct? Correct? Correct? Hmm," he again pinched his chin, "Ahh... An analytic insight. You are rather beset by an anxiety attack. After all," he pointed upward. "My method of exculpating your grandson is a double-edged sword. Hypnosis may instead convict Geoffrey of the heinous deed. Then your endeavor wouldn't just roll back down the hill like a Sisyphean rock, but would fall into an abyss and be eternally sealed."

"No."

"No?" The psychiatrist's jaw dropped.

"No. I have complete faith in Geoff. It's the rest of my family that concerns me. Over Christmas, Dolly and I experienced an alarming episode with Geoffrey's younger brother, Myles."

"Ahh, I never actually met Myles, although his mother did elucidate on the fraternal discord between him and Geoffrey. Your daughter indicated that Geoffrey was always the instigator."

"Lenore saying that doesn't surprise me at all. But I found her reaction to this incident involving Myles as most peculiar. Not only did she refuse to hear about it, but after suggesting they both consult you, she became indignant. I am equally troubled over them both."

"What happened?" Dr. Tryvye spread his palms.

Looking at Geoffrey, Norman, and Victor, Scotch put his hand on the psychiatrist's shoulder. "I'd rather not discuss it here. Make an appointment for me. I'd rather talk in the privacy of your office."

"Very well. I'll set aside fifty-minutes, I mean, an hour for you."

# Chapter 19

Elizabeth and Marion Endicott sat in the King Henry room of the Windsor Cricket Club. They sipped pink sherry from long-stemmed crystal goblets.

Martin reluctantly approached the table. "Um, excuse me, my profuse apologies for interrupting," Martin's right arm crossed to his left wrist, "but, um," he fidgeted with his watch.

Marion pierced Martin with his dilated pupils, grinned, then winked. Elizabeth strummed her fingers on the tabletop.

"Yes, Liz." Martin smiled. "A Mr. Slovo from the Odyssey Corporation to see you. He says you're expecting him."

The socialite nodded toward the door. Martin motioned to the executive.

Briefcase in hand, Peter Slovo waltzed to the Endicotts' table. He hesitated before sitting. Marion and Petermade eye contact Instant animosity. The socialite's son glowered at the businessman's leering, acne-scarred face and stood. The words, '*What's the matter? Afraid that I might actually desire your fat, ugly, aging body?*" lingered between his mind and tongue.

Without invite, Peter Slovo took a seat next to Elizabeth and across from Marion. He just as quickly spread several briefs and blueprints on the table. He leaned toward the socialite. "The first thing we must abandon is the myth that a Norman Rockwell Americana ever existed. It never had and it never will. Leave Hometown, U.S.A. to Disney Land. Stanforth has, for too long, clung to such archaic fancy. The result is an economic and architectural stagnation that has made the area an outmoded and inconvenient place to live. My plan will put the Stanforth area on the highway to the twenty-first century. Would you agree that a major problem facing Stanforth is inaccessibility?"

Elizabeth nodded.

"As we all know, Stanforth lies a tangle and maze of stoplights and local lanes from both the Pennsylvania Turnpike and the Schuylkill Expressway. The first step is to build a limited-access highway linking the Pennsylvania Turnpike and the Schuylkill Expressway to Interstate Route 95. Your husband is very close to Governor Stanton. Your other son," Peter winced at Marion, "Mitchell, is among other things, a well-connected state senator. Surely your influence can make that proposal a reality."

"How will Stanforth benefit from another highway?" Elizabeth asked.

"Accessibility." Peter pointed upward. "Lancaster Avenue is the key. As you know, the proposed highway will cut across

Yorkshire Township. You also know that Lancaster Avenue was never intended as a town boulevard. When built in the eighteenth century, Lancaster Avenue was a prototype of the modern expressway. Ironic, isn't it?" Peter chuckled. "Here I'm asking you to forsake a pre-World War I romantic notion, yet embrace a Pre-Revolutionary intention. So therefore let's fulfill Lancaster Avenue's original purpose and make it a limited-access expressway and serve as the new highway's aorta."

"How can that be achieved?" Elbow on table, Elizabeth rested chin on thumb, forefinger bracing cheek.

"With your influence, easily. First, expand Lancaster Avenue to six lanes. Second, bridge over, tunnel under, or block all intersecting local roads. Third, eliminate all access save strategic high-speed merges."

Elizabeth rested her forearms on the table and steepled her fingers. "But Stanforth and the Main Line towns lack the space to expand Lancaster Avenue to six lanes."

"Eminent domain."

"Eminent domain?"

"Yes, eminent domain." Peter Slovo put his hands, palms down, on the table. "If the government deems it in the public good to appropriate private property..."

"I know what eminent domain means." Elizabeth pinched her chin.

"Then the solution is simple." Peter Slovo softly punched the tabletop. "Lean on Governor Stanton to condemn the properties flanking Lancaster Avenue. After all, you'll be doing the proprietors a favor, getting their tired, overworked butts out of Pennsylvania's cold weather and into comfortable retirement in sunny Florida. You as a Bechtel Corporation board member should know." Peter Slovo raised his hands, "small, independently-owned businesses are passé. Corporate enterprise is the wave of the future. Now is the time to catch that wave. Introducing the new Stanforth." The Odyssey executive shoved a blueprint before Elizabeth. "Most of Stanforth's Victorian storefronts were built at the time of the Ford Model T. Coincidently, most of the Paoli Local's coaches were manufactured at the same time. That should tell you that Stanforth no longer needs rail transportation. The automobile, on the other hand, has advanced considerably since then. Now don't you think it's high time Stanforth does likewise? By leveling Stanforth's faded, decaying old storefronts, as well as tearing up the sidewalks in front and the little lane in back, we can indeed expand Lancaster Avenue to six lanes, and," Peter Slovo beamed, "have room enough left over to replace them with these sparkling Bauhaus structures." He pointed to an illustration of square, flat-roofed buildings on concrete stilts. "These new commercial buildings will provide nearly twice the floor space of Stanforth's now antiquated shops. The mirrored glass exterior of Stanforth's new outlets will make for more efficient climate control. Best of all is accessibility. You will agree that parking is a major problem in Stanforth."

Elizabeth Endicott nodded.

"Even worse," Peter Slovo continued, "is scrounging for nickels to stick in those damn parking meters, and nobody, but nobody, likes getting shafted with a two-dollar parking ticket. Odyssey's plan eliminates parking meters altogether. In fact, by building the stores on stilts, the consumer will get three additional rows of free parking. Notice the escalators?" The executive tapped the blueprint. "Now consumers can zoom off Lancaster Expressway's access lane, zip their cars right in, jump right out, and ride right up. You can imagine that a lot more merchandise will turn over. That will mean greater profits. Greater profits mean higher property valuations. Higher property valuations mean higher taxes. Higher taxes mean more money in Stanforth's coffers."

"Wait a minute," Marion interjected. "I see where you've turned the intersection of Lancaster Avenue and North and South Stanforth Avenues into an overpass with high-speed entrance ramps. Won't that eat up a lot of space for shops?"

"Ahh ... " Peter Slovo held up his hand. "Think of it as a few doors closing so that many more can open. Introducing Odyssey's most exciting proposal." The executive opened a folder. "Odyssey Mall! Utilizing 200 acres of worthless forest and meadow, our mega mall will provide nearly two million square feet of shopping convenience. You see, Marion, South and North Stanforth Avenues will become an arterial highway that will direct consumers to Odyssey Mall and its 3,000 free parking spaces. Nearly every corporate retail chain in the United States will be represented here."

Elizabeth sipped her sherry. "I applaud your enthusiasm. Nevertheless, Stanforth lacks the population base to support such an ambitious project."

"It doesn't have to be that way." Peter Slovo rapped the tabletop. "I see where Yorkshire Township has several working farms. Another unprofitable obsolescence. Use your influence to rezone that land as commercial. By increasing their property taxes by quantum leaps, the old relics will beg us for an offer." He opened another folder. "Odyssey Corporation proposes to use that land for these major tract home developments." He laid three sets of illustrations before Mrs. Endicott. "Shady Grove. Elysian Fields. And Country Estates. All conveniently connected to the new Lancaster Expressway."

"Unfortunately, Mr. Slovo, Yorkshire High School can only

accommodate about a thousand students tops."

"Yorkshire High School is also badly located."

"Its downtown position," Elizabeth Endicott raised her steepled fingers, "allows most of our students to walk to school."

"It also limits space for athletic fields. Maybe that's why your football team hasn't enjoyed a winning season since Lance Burkett."

"Lance Burkett, huh." The socialite placed her folded arms on the table. "I applaud you, Mr. Slovo, for doing your homework on Stanforth's history."

"It's my job to care about your community. I'll prove to you just how much Odyssey cares. If the state of Pennsylvania will play ball with us, Mrs. Endicott, Odyssey Corporation will help build Yorkshire Township a new 5,000-student capacity high school, complete with athletic fields, on the fringes of Odyssey Mall." Slovo pointed upward. "That is only the beginning! With our plan, Yorkshire Township will soon attract high tax-paying light industry and office complexes. And just think of the additional revenue the Township can collect by renting billboard space along the new highways."

"You do present a workable scheme." Elizabeth Endicott nodded. "Moreover, I can foresee its profitability. Nevertheless, Mr. Slovo," Elizabeth Endicott aimed her steepled fingers at him. "I harbor some reservations. First of all..."

Marion interrupted, "I find your plan revolt ..."

Elizabeth held her hand up to her son. "You speak with an accent, Mr. Slovo. You're not American, are you?"

"Dutch."

"And Odyssey Corporation. Chicago-based. Correct?"

"Correct, Mrs. Endicott."

"Okay, so Yorkshire Township will gain additional tax revenue from all off this." Elizabeth tapped one of the blueprints. "Yet the private earnings of Yorkshire's residents, as well as any other money spent at your new stores, mega mall, or on one of your housing developments, won't it all get siphoned away to Chicago?"

Peter Slovo furtively glanced about the room; then he leaned closer to the socialite and spoke with faint voice and minimal lip movement. "Look. Odyssey never intended our presentation to appeal solely to your sense of civic duty or social conscience. Come through for us on this, Mrs. Endicott. Put the Governor in our pocket. Rally the state legislature to our side. And you're in for a commission. A tidy commission."

"Well, Mr. Slovo, on a decision of this magnitude, I think it best I get a second opinion; don't you?" Elizabeth nodded at the door.

An ashen Betty Kirby stood in the doorway, a clattering jaw her only indication of being alive.

"I'm glad you kept your appointment. Come." The committee president beckoned her minion to the table.

Betty stumbled in like a stickman.

Elizabeth motioned to a chair.

Betty anxiously obliged.

"Mrs. Kirby," Elizabeth continued. "I'd like you to meet a Mr. Peter Slovo of the Odyssey Corporation. He proposes expanding Lancaster Avenue into a six-lane expressway. Then they'll bulldoze Stanforth's central business district and replace it with this." Elizabeth pointed to the Bauhaus sketches. "His new Lancaster Expressway will feed these projected tributary highways." She ran her finger along a map. "They will lead to their two-million-square-foot mega-mall proposed for the wooded fringes of Valley Forge National Park. His plan also includes these," she thrice tapped the map, "three sprawling tract housing developments. What do you think, Betty?" Elizabeth smiled and nodded.

"Yes." Betty fidgeted with her wedding ring. "I like it."

"You do? Very good." Elizabeth squeezed Betty's hand. "I'm glad." Betty sighed and smiled.

"Because I was concerned as to whether or not, as I heard you suggest, I truly am crazy." Betty gasped.

"Since it's two to one against. I guess it's confirmed that I am. I'm relieved. Now I can seek the appropriate treatment. On the other hand ... Marion. What do you think?"

Marion stood and squared his feet. "I may have to agree with you, Mr. Slovo, about the impossibility of restoring Norman Rockwell's vision of community-- but I'd take Edward Hopper's America over your abomination any day."

"Martin. What do you think?" Elizabeth asked.

"Uww...Yech!" Martin leaned over the proposal and bobbed his finger in his mouth, pretending to puke. Afterwards he wrapped his arm around Marion's back. They touched heads.

Peter Slovo stood with jittering finger. "But they're a couple of ... "

"Clark. Come on over." Elizabeth beckoned to the golfer wearing purple knickers, green shirt with white sleeves, and pink cap. "How long have you been married?"

"Twenty-eight years."

"How many kids?"

"Two sons, a daughter, and eight grandchildren."

"What do you think of this scheme?"

"Ha! Ha! Ha!" Clarkson Meredith Walden feigned swatting away the plans with his gold putter.

"Oh come on." Peter held up his hands. "Look at him. He's dressed like a freakin' ... "

Elizabeth stood and pinched the collar of her olive green, custom-tailored executive jacket.

"Mr. Slovo, I see no compelling reason to prolong this meeting. And Mrs. Kirby. Seeing that one of us is crazy, and that it's not I. I think a little rest and recuperation would do you a world of good. Therefore, I want to do my part in helping you. I'm relieving you of the stress and strain of a committee member's burden."

"But. But. But." Betty started to tic.

"Martin. Please summon security. Have them show Mr. Slovo and Mrs. Kirby the door."

"Lenore's behind this," Betty grumbled. "It's Lenore," she spoke. "Isn't it?" Betty shrieked and jabbed her finger at the committee president. "Isn't it!"

"It's Lenore...Lenore. Lenore! Lenore!" Betty Kirby

continued to shout that name as a beefy security guard wrestled her

out the door.

# Chapter 20

"That's it, Geoffrey," Dr. Tryvye leaned forward. "Stay relaxed. Lie back and relax. Think of nothing at all. Just let your eyes follow the pendulum. Think of nothing, nothing at all... Just watch the pendulum sway back and forth, back and forth..."

The psychiatrist observed that the boy's orbs followed the pendulum, while his pupils remained fixed.

"O.K. Geoffrey, I think you're ready... Ready to go on an adventure. A journey. A voyage to the realm of the subconscious mind. In the subconscious mind, anything is possible. Even a trip back in time. You're returning to that horrible Monday afternoon in early November. That final day before arriving at Harlond State. Geoffrey, you have two subconscious minds. With one you will relive that afternoon. With the other you will observe and report to me what is happening, sort of like broadcasting a Phillies or Eagles game. Geoffrey, go back, back in time... That's it... Can you see yourself in the family room?"

"Yes."

"What exactly do you see?"

"I see myself looking in a book. I'm imagining myself in a spaceship rocketing along Saturn's rings."

"Very good, Geoffrey. Now what do you hear?"

"Just Myles and Donald playing... Wait... I hear my Lee Lee cat crying. Now my father is yelling... I'm running to the dining room..."

"What do you see in the dining room?"

"Lee Lee! No! She's dead!"

"And your father?"

"He killed her. *He* killed her!"

"Is he sorry?"

"No. He's angry. Angry at me. He's yelling at me."

"What's he yelling?"

"It wouldn't have happened if you listened and kept the damn animal outside... He's pointing at me. He's got a mean face and he's pointing at me."

"What's he saying to you, Geoffrey?"

"Let this be a lesson. Now get that damn thing out of here before I do the same to you."

"And you Geoffrey. What did you do?"

"Ahhh!" Geoffrey screamed. "I'm hitting him with a chair!"

"Do you feel bad about doing this?"

"No! He killed Lee Lee. He deserves it."

"Does he deserve to die, Geoffrey?"

"Yes! He deserves to die!" Geoffrey growled, his face twisting diabolically.

Dr. Tryvye gasped. He stood, walked over and looked out a window. Composing himself, he checked the tape recorder's gauges, took a deep breath, and sat down.

"Okay, Geoff. It's all right...It's all right for you to feel that way. Relax. Relax. Tell me what you did next?"

"Nothing. I can't do nothing."

"Why can't you, Geoffrey?"

"My father's got me wrapped up. He's beating me. He's slamming my head against the wall. He looks so angry... So mad..." Geoffrey passed out.

"Geoffrey. Listen. I want you to open your eyes and look at the pendulum."

Geoffrey awakened.

"Very good Geoffrey. Now don't worry... Just follow the pendulum... Nobody is mad at you. You won't get in any trouble. All you have to do is tell me what you did next."

"The closet. Just darkness. The closet is so dark..." Geoffrey again lost consciousness.

"Come back Geoffrey. That's it. Don't stop looking at the pendulum. Very good. The ax. Do you remember an ax?"

"No ax. I can't remember anything. Just the closet. The dark closet."

"Don't go back to sleep. Go back to the closet, but try to stay awake. You can stay awake. You can remember leaving the closet."

"Yes. But it hurts."

"What hurts?"

"My arm. Someone's twisting my arm."

"Pretend that you can float, that will make the hurt go away... Very good, Geoffrey... You're now hovering above like the blimp that floats over the football games. What do you see happening to yourself? Can you tell me who is hurting your arm?"

"A policeman. I see a policeman twisting my arm and putting handcuffs on me... There!... I see the ax you asked me about. Another policeman is putting it in a bag."

"Did you ever use that ax?"

"No. I only see the policeman putting it in a plastic bag. Now they're carrying me away. Away..." Geoffrey started losing consciousness. "Stay awake Geoffrey. Try and stay awake. You can do it... Very good. What do you remember next?"

"Here."

"Here?"

"Yes. Here. Harlond State. A jail cell in Harlond State."

"Did you kill your father with the ax that the policeman put in the plastic bag?"

"No... No... No... I never killed my father."

"But you said he deserved to die?"

"Yes... He killed my Lee Lee cat... He was always cruel to me... Beat me... Called me horrible names... But I didn't kill him... I only hit him with a chair, then I woke up here... Here. Only then did you tell me he was dead and that I did it."

"How did that make you feel?"

"No good... No good... But he killed my Lee Lee. I want my Lee Lee cat." Geoff started crying.

"It's okay Geoffrey. Lee Lee is alive. She survived the incident. You never have to be angry at your father again. He's gone. I'm going to bring you back to the present. You're going to return to your conscious mind. Now I'm turning off the pendulum... When I clap my hands you will awaken. All you will remember is that you never have to be angry at your father again."

Three seconds later, Dr. Tryvye clapped.

Geoff awoke with a start; his head bobbed as if he had a spring for a neck.

"How do you feel Geoffrey?"

"Tired." Geoff rubbed his eyes. "Like awakening from a deep sleep. You know, time seems to have passed in a flash, but you still know that many hours went by."

"That's good Geoffrey." Dr. Tryvye pinched his goatee. "You did very good."

"Now do you believe me?" Geoff stood and spread his arms. "When can I go live with Grand-dad?"

"Later, Geoffrey, we'll talk about it later. It's time to go back to your room."

"But I don't wanna go back to my room! I wanna go to grand-dad's farm. I don't wanna stay here. I hate it here!"

Dr. Tryvye nodded to Victor Washington.

The orderly gently secured Geoffrey's arm. "Come on, Geoffrey. I know ya want out. But I'm afraid that you gotta come with me. You can take it just a little while longer."

"How much longer? I don't wanna go back. I'm sick of this place."

Victor dragged the crying boy away. Dr. Tryvye sat behind his desk, pulled some forms from a drawer, and scribbled in them.

"Let me go!" Geoff struggled in Victor's grip. "This is no fair! I'm sick of this place." The boy struggled harder. "I didn't do nothing wrong! I don't deserve no more of this. Now let me go home to Grand-dad."

"You know I can't do that." Victor pulled a feet-dragging Geoffrey down the hallway. "Come on now, don't hassle me. I'm just doing my job."

"No! No! Let me go! I'm sick of this place. I did nothing wrong. I didn't do nothin to deserve gettin' punished in the first place. So why are ya still doin' it to me? This ain't fair. No Fair!" Geoff's resistance proved futile against the powerful orderly. He remained silent as the orderly dragged him closer to his room.

A nurse emerged. "You can let him go, Victor. He has a phone call." She looked at Geoff. "Over here." The nurse pointed to the reception desk.

Victor released his grip. Geoffrey ran to the reception desk. He yanked the receiver from the nurse's hand. "Hello? Hello?"

"Why hello there, Geoff. How ya do?"

"Norman! They won't let me go. I'm sick of this place. This is all no fair!"

"I know. I know, Geoffi-ey. Many things in life are unfair. You've got to have faith like Job and Apostle Paul and believe that God is using this to prepare ya for somethin' great."

"But I'm just a kid. This is all no fair."

"Hey. Baby Moses and Baby Jesus had to be hidden from evil people who wanted to kill 'em. Was that fair? I know it's no good that you never got to be a kid, but I just know God wants to make ya into a great man. After all, all things work together for the good of those who love the Lord."

"How many times have ya told me that before? Well, I hate the Lord for makin' me stay here!" Geoff banged the phone on the desk.

"Hey! Hey! Now I know that ain't you speakin'. Sounds more like a demon. That don't surprise me none. There's got to be lots'a those where you are. But right now as I speak, Jesus himself is chasing all those demons away."

Geoffrey heaved three deep breaths. "I'm sorry Norman. I don't hate God. I don't know what made me say that. Can he forgive me?"

"Your Lord Jesus forgives everything. But don't be sayin' his name in vain no more, okay? He takes that very seriously, ya know."

"I'm sorry Norman." Geoff wiped away a tear, then sniffled. Suddenly bile rose from his stomach. He tensed his lips and growled, "But I do hate my damn parents for what they did to me! And daddy deserved to die for all he did. What do you have to say about that? 'Honor thy mother and Father'?"

"Hey, hey. Enough of that. Jesus can chase away those demons, but if ya let 'em come back, they will. And seven times stronger and meaner. But I will answer your question." Norman paused for effect. "No." He was silent for seven seconds. "In fact, Christ said, 'He who loves his father or mother more than me is not worthy of me'."

"There! You see! Jesus knew some kids would get shafted with parents like mine."

"Oh no, Geoffrey, that ain't what he be sayin' at all."

"But you just said that Jesus said..."

"Jesus didn't say to not love your mom and dad. He only said that you're to love them more. Than him. Geoffrey, if you don't love your parents at all, how much can ya love Jesus?"

Geoffrey sniffled.

"Well, Geoffrey, Jesus says that if you love him, obey his

commandments. And does not Jesus command you to honor your mother and father?"

"Yes. But..."

"But nothin.' I told you before, Jesus even extended love to those that beat and killed him. How can Jesus live in your heart if you're full 'a hate? Obey his commandment by getting the hate outta your heart. Keepin' hatred can only hurt you."

"But this is no fair! I don't deserve getting locked up in this place." Geoffrey broke down.

"Did Jesus deserve what he got? Did Job? Millions of people have it far worse than you right now."

"You just don't understand!" The boy shouted through his tears.

"I don't? Why don't you try goin' through life on one leg and livin' in a tar paper shack. You're only thirteen. You've got your entire life ahead of ya. God gave ya the gifts to accomplish great things. Before that happens though, you've got to get hate out of your heart. Then you can take charge of your life and move forward."

"I think I'm startin' to understand."

"I think you are too," Norman replied.

"Thank you Norman. I love you Norman."

"I loves ya too, Geoff. Ya know somethin'? I sense Jesus's presence. He's gonna bring us all together again. Soon. Geoff. Soon. 'Til then, keep that faith and hope, and most important, love."

Geoffrey shrugged.

"I'm afraid time is up. I'm sorry, Geoffrey." Dr. Tryvye cuffed his arm. "It's time to go back to your room."

Geoff calmly returned to his room.

# Chapter 21

Sitting next to her Prince Charming, Lenore felt like Cinderella riding the enchanted chariot to the royal ball. Wayne Madison's Ferrari, of course, packed far more than just a team of metamorphosed mice under its hood. Additionally, the grandeur of the Endicotts' Shakespearean manor house matched any storybook castle's. After Wayne yielded his Italian sports car to the valet so that it could join the fleet of dormant Rolls Royces, Bentleys, Mercedes limousines, and other cars costing more than a four-bedroom Bluffington house, he waltzed Lenore into the Endicotts' main vestibule.

Earlier, Marion Endicott supervised converting the manor's reception rooms from cozy Anglo-Saxon traditional to open Greco-Roman classical. That motif better suited two hundred New Year's Eve party guests. Marion placed several of his sculptures atop Greek Doric, Ionic, and Corinthian pedestals to perfect the aura. Lenore, hearing her spiked heels click on the floor of colored marble laid like Ravenna mosaics, realized the impossibility of glass slippers. Yet on Wayne's arm, she felt as if balancing upon a rainbow. After all, upon crossing the Endicotts' threshold, their sweeping, brass-railed main staircase impressed her as an ascent to paradise.

The scale of the Endicotts' reception rooms bedazzled her.

The occasion uplifted Lenore enough for her to chuckle at an otherwise unpleasant New Year's Eve memory...

...Pat Huggins's three-bedroom Bluffington hovel could easily fit into the Endicotts' main vestibule. Lenore had to endure insufferable wives' chit-chat while her husband drank beer, talked sports, and told dirty jokes to his male buddies. Four... Three... Two... One... Midnight at last. Lenore, after hours of lonely boredom, actually desired a kiss from her husband. She strode to within six inches of Lance... Pat Huggins suddenly announced, "Look at me!" He dumped the bourbon-spiked contents of a punch bowl on his head. "Happy New Year!" Wearing the bowl like a helmet, Pat Huggins banged a ladle on it while singing, "Auld Lang Syne". Instead of kissing his wife, Lance slapped backs with Eddie Krause and Paul Barton. They laughed as if Pat's antics were the most creative and funny sight they'd ever seen..

...Cinderella had an evil stepmother and two evil stepsisters to contend with. Yet Princess Lenore, by entwining arms with Prince Wayne, Elizabeth Endicott was the Queen of the ball rather than an evil stepmother. While smiling and exchanging niceties, Lenore scanned about for evil stepsister number one. No sign of Betty Kirby. Lenore gloated. Wayne then introduced her to Governor Stanton. She acquitted herself with nouveau savoir-faire as they exchanged obeisances. Schiller Sterling soon joined them. Lenore wandered off as the diplomat and her prince excluded her from their arcane public policy discussion.

A French drop-side sofa fronted double stained glass windows. The windows' Renaissance motif was draped by Louis XVI period silk. Estelle Endicott scrunched into the sofa's sole backrest. Hillary Sterling held Estelle's wrist and put her hand in her son Cornelius's hand. "Oh, Niely." Hillary squeezed her son's free hand. "Ask Estelle about her youth committee. It's a rousing success as I know you two will be as a couple."

Cornelius held his mother's hand while looking around for Marion Endicott. Lenore looped in for a closer look closer. Hillary released her grip on Estelle and her son to scowl and curl her lip at Lenore. Cornelius Sterling exploited those unguarded seconds to sneak away. Hillary spotted her son fleeing. She marched like a Teamster about to confront a scab toward the woman who dashed her plans. "You never met Dorothy Madison; did you? Well, let me tell you something: she was a saint. But you? Ugh! Right now she must be spinning in her grave."

Hillary's words rankled Lenore like a flag burning would a Veteran of Foreign Wars member. She unsheathed her fingernails. Hillary cocked her slapping hand.

"There you are." Wayne Madison wrapped his arm around

Lenore. "I was wondering where you gamboled off to. Ahhh... Mrs. Sterling. What a delight. Enjoying the evening?"

Hillary gasped as her rival snuggled against the Cricket Club President. Mrs. Sterling then licked two fingers and kneaded her makeup. "Of course, Wayne. Would an Endicott gala ever fall short of exquisite? And the hor d'oeuvres. Absolutely delectable." She signaled to a black-tied waiter and took a toothpicked tidbit from his gold platter. "Mmmm." She nibbled. "Pollo Fra Diavolo." Hillary licked her fingers. "That's *farm-raised chicken* in a spicy tomato sauce".

Lenore and Hillary crossed eyes at each other.

* * *

Check Sutton's feet crunched in the broken glass. Shaka kicked aside an empty beer can. He glanced at it rattling along the cracked sidewalk.

"We're here." Check pointed to a door painted sky blue with a sun-like eye penetrating a cloud.

"All right, brother." Shaka slapped Check's hand. "Hey, can we start the new decade any way else but flying high?"

"Not so fast, gentlemen." A thirty-year-old Black male stepped in front of them. Check, flummoxed, skewed his head. This door guard stood no taller than himself. Moreover, he possessed a handsome, clean-cut, and unscarred face.

"What's the magic word?"

"Hey, what it is, bro." Shaka held his hand out.

"Not quite." The door guard put his hands in the pockets of his army surplus field jacket and blocked the doorway with his extended elbows.

"All is one?" Check squeaked.

The guard stepped aside and opened the painted door. Shaka avidly negotiated the creaky stairs. Check gingerly followed. The new cleanliness of the otherwise dilapidated interior puzzled him. Finding the door to Father's apartment open, they warily looked at one another. Finally, Check shrugged and led Shaka into the flat.

"Come this way," said an unseen voice. Check sighed relief and spread apart the same strings of beads and sea shells for Shaka. They entered.

An Asian Indian clad in a white robe and matching white turban awaited them. He sat cross-kneed on Fafner's old Persian pillow. Check smiled on recognizing Fafner's wall paintings of blue-skinned, rat, and monkey-faced humanoids.

"Greetings, acolytes. Peace." The Indian raised his hands with forefinger and middle finger extended in the era's "peace sign".

"Peace." Check returned the gesture. "But where's Fafner?"

"Fafner was taken away on a pilgrimage. There, he is learning the true meaning of social justice. I, the Swami Maharajah Yogi, am now your spiritual intercessor. Sit, my children." He nodded at two Persian pillows. Check and Shaka sat.

"May the light illuminate and enrich you. The light of the blue moon. May it put a dream in your heart and bring you a love of your own. Ahhh... The light is bringing me a spiritual revelation." The Swami made two peace signs, closed his eyes, and chanted: "Sha-na-na-na; sha-na-na; bop-shu-bop; bop-shu-bop." He opened his eyes. "Wop-bop-a-lu-bop-a-wop-bam-boom. The light grants an epiphany." He reached behind himself and presented a brass tray with two twenty-dollar bills. "Your seeds of the great transformation no longer bear fruit. Exchange them now, so that I, the Swami Maharajah Yogi, can provide you with fertile seeds to plant the new decade's, new order."

Check placed a clear plastic bag with several pills on the tray. Shaka added a foil pouch of cannabis to the platter. They each took twenty dollars.

The Swami again made two peace signs, closed his eyes, and chanted. "Bop-shu-bop; rama-lama-ding dong; dip; dip, dip; dip; dip, dip." He pulled from his robe two bags of white powder and placed them on the tray. "Here, my acolytes. The rejuvenated seeds of the great transformation. Place ninety dollars each on the tray and take them. Bring peace on Earth and goodwill to men."

Check and Shaka's addition totaled the two-twenties, plus two tens, four fives, three ones, eight quarters, two dimes, and a nickel.

The Swami clenched the bills in his right hand and the coins in his left. He then closed his eyes and chanted. "Bomp-bomp-bomp. Boogie, boogie, boogie, da shoop. 'Till these notes turn to dust; 'till these coins turn to rust... You two will be rotting in jail... This is a bust."

"What?" Check stood and pointed with a jittery finger. "Hey, man! Get off me!" He protested as two uniformed policemen bolted in, wrestled his arms behind his back, and handcuffed him.

The Black 'door guard' entered and flashed his detective badge. "You have the right to remain silent. Anything you say can and will be used against you..."

"Come-on. brother," a handcuffed Shaka said from the clutches of two cops. "Be cool. Let's talk about this. We can make a deal."

"I'm not your brother," the detective replied. "The only deals you'll be cutting will be with the D.A.. Anything you say can and will be..."

* * *

The Dave Brubeck Quartet featuring Joe Morello on the drums played in the Endicott's far south reception hall. Lenore and Wayne waltzed in the more intimate north reception hall to a chamber orchestra's rendition of the barcarolle from Jacques Offenbach's *Les contes d'Hoffmann.* "Um, excuse me, Mrs. Burkett."

Lenore turned her head to the tap on her shoulder. She spotted a liveried servant holding a silver charger with an early twentieth-century brass and ivory telephone. "A phone call for you."

"Who is it from?" Lenore slipped from Wayne's flowing embrace. "He didn't say. But he did say that it was of utmost urgency."

Lenore looked at Wayne. "It's probably just Myles." She put the receiver to her ear. "Yes."

"Sis. It's me?"

"Check! Is that you?" She turned away from Wayne and covered the mouthpiece.

"Yeah, it's me. Look, I need…"

"Where on Earth have you been?"

"Hey, sis, it's like, I couldn't deal with that fascist pig husband of yours, so I split for the village."

"Greenwich Village?"

"Yeah, Listen. Ya gotta give me..."

"How did you get this number?"

"Myles. Look, I'm damn lucky the pigs are letting me make a second phone call."

"Pigs? Where are you now?"

"At the pig station. I got busted. Now look, ya gotta.."

"Police station?"

"Yeah. The pig house. The pokey. Look, it's like this, the pigs busted me in a sting operation. My bail's five grand. Myles told me you're seeing Wayne Madison. I can't believe it. Groovy man. He's got more bread than Stanforth's wealthiest capitalist pig. Have him give me five grand to get me outta the joint, then another five grand to tide me over in Canada."

"Canada?"

"Yeah, Canada. If the pigs can pin this rap on me, and you can bet your sweet hippy they will, they're gonna make me join the Army. Do understand? The Army! Now that is like, one real bad trip. If ya know what I mean."

"Why didn't you come to my husband's funeral? You could've at least called."

"Come on, sis. Your husband was a drag. I figured you threw a party to celebrate being rid of him. Seeing that I was doin' some heavy partying of my own up here in the village, I decided to take a pass. Hey, like, didn't I always tell you that Geoffrey was a rotten apple? Anyway. Wayne Madison. Far out. Like, what more could ya ask for? Ten grand is peanuts to him. So how-a-bout-it, sis?"

"So my husband was a drag, huh? Well, he was right about one thing."

"What's that sis?"

"That you do need to grow a pair of balls. And who can make you grow 'em better than the Army." Lenore hung up the phone and excused the butler.

"Who was that?" Wayne asked.

"Just Myles. He was only checking up on me. You know how he is." Lenore started gasping. She felt a bead of sweat flowing down her cheek and brow. After touching herself beneath the eye, she blanched at the sight of a viscous eye shadow on her fingers. Urgently she turned away from Wayne. "You'll have to excuse me. Got to run to the powder room. A woman's thing, you know."

Three minutes later, Lenore found the Endicott's main

powder room. Three weeks later, a shorn Check Sutton was counting his push-ups: "One drill sergeant, two drill sergeant, three drill sergeant..."

"Out-of-the-way. Got an emergency." A bowling ball-bodied woman in her late fifties, topped by an orange derby straight from the mad hatter, bumped Lenore aside and commandeered the powder room.

After five helpless, makeup-dripping minutes of standing by the locked door, Lenore started searching for an alternate powder room. She covered her face with her hands while straddling the corridor wall en route to a rear stairway. On the second floor, her search for a powder room took her past an apparent bedroom door. A curious sound. No. A distinct sound. Sexual moans. Lenore put her ear to the door and heard: "Oh, oh, I love you, Endicott." She peeped through the keyhole and smiled broader than a quarter moon. The anticipation of casting torment upon her enemy tasted aambrosial. Lenore licked her lips. Each step toward the party felt as ascending a level to Nirvana. Yet her feet felt light not. Their heaviness buoyed her with pulverizing power, as if wearing boots of iron driven by nuclear-powered pistons. For her vengeance feast will devour more than just flesh and blood. It will charge her with the capacity to crush her foe underfoot. Her fingertips tingled. She felt a surge swell her muscles. Her mind felt lucid, avenues opened in every direction, yet she commanded the facility to choose the perfect path. "Oh, Hillary." Lenore held her hand.

Mrs. Sterling reflexively retracted it and sneered.

"I have the most wonderful news for you. I was just upstairs..."

Hillary looked about. "Look, Miss Sutton, Mrs. Burkett, or whatever you go by these days. The only wonderful news you could ever bring me, and yourself for that matter…"

Lenore shrank as she pictured two clucking chickens running figure eight around her and Hillary's ankles. Suddenly one transmuted into a vulture, the second a raven. Each then perched upon one of Lenore's shoulders and sized up her snotty opponent. The vulture's rigid, wisp-like tongue licked its scabrous beak. Lenore suppressed laughter. Both at visions of Hillary's impending ruin and the silliness of her clichéd imagination. The raven looked at Hillary Sterling and said: *'Nevermore.'* "Sutton? Burkett? What will you care when the connection is Sterling, Endicott? Oh, Hillary now that your families are combining you'll be invincible," Lenore slumped. "Won't you please show me mercy? Please forgive me for what I was born into and allow me to serve under you."

Hillary stood erect, placed hands on hips, and focused downward. "What on Earth are you talking about?"

"Your son and that most eligible of Endicotts. When they disappeared, where do you think they went? Oh, Hillary. I saw them together. Their love has overwhelmed and humbled me. Your families joining forces has shown me my place." Lenore retook Hillary's hand and lowered her head.

That boosted Hillary like a child getting her first hint that a long-wanted pony is her Christmas present. "You mean, my Niely and the Endicotts...?"

"Yes." Lenore interrupted. "Your Cornelius. I was up on the second floor. I walked past the white bedroom door with the brass and marble doorknob. Oh, Hillary. They're together and so much in love."

"My Niely... My Niely and Elizabeth Endicott's own." Mrs. Sterling trotted up the sweeping main staircase like Pegasus in a cloud. Lenore shadowed her furtively as a Bond villain. Hillary Sterling glued her ear to the white bedroom door's keyhole. Lenore pressed her left fist against her forehead, clenched her teeth, and contracted her lips, attempting to stifle laughter.

"Oh, Endicott...I love you; I love you; I love you. I love it; I love it; I love it."

Cornelius Sterling's moans of lust rather than affection failed to make his mother suspicious. He was making love to an Endicott!

And nothing else mattered. "Keep doing me...Big boy."

Well ...Almost.

"Huh," Hillary gasped. She barged open the door urgently as if her baby were on fire. "No..." She covered her eyes. Although her heart stopped pumping blood, her tear ducts forced brine between her taut fingers like sea water driven through cracks in a dyke. "No. No. No. No. No." A tormented moment later, she uncovered her eyes. Hazy vision prevented accurate perception. That allowed her breathing and heartbeat to stabilize. Standing relaxed, her eyes started focusing. "Ahhhh!" she screamed. Her dearest son was naked atop a bed. Down on his forearms and knees, he had his buttocks raised to accommodate a nude Marion Endicott's thrusting hips. His entire penis appeared and disappeared from her son's rectum like a piston in and out of a crankcase. "Uhhh," his mother groaned as her heart burned into her stomach like a habanero-spiced meatball. A gaping Hillary now stood pallid and still as a snowman.

"Oh, mom." Cornelius turned his head to his mother. "You're always interfering with my fun."

Hillary and her son's lover then glared at each other maliciously. "Look, woman. Shows over. Now make like a banana and split." Marion leaned over, wrapped his arms around Cornelius's waist, and rested his head on his back, facing Hillary.

"And close the door behind you."

"That ... That ... That," she muttered. Her snowy face reddened like Rudolph the reindeer's nose. "Bitch!" Hillary clenched her fists and contorted her face. Then she stormed from the bedroom, charged down the stairs, marched across the vestibule, and confronted the corrupting queer's mother. After a three-second glower, Hillary spat in Elizabeth Endicott's face. Briskly Mrs. Sterling slapped her.

The party banter silenced. Circular-mouthed guests stared at the scene. Before they could conceive the inconceivable, Elizabeth Endicott wiped the phlegm from her stinging cheek and calmly retreated to her private parlor. Several phone calls later, Hillary Sterling was removed from every social register in the United States.

Hillary stomped out the door and slammed it behind her. Schiller gave chase. Mrs. Sterling's next societal appearance would be at a reception celebrating her husband's arrival at his new diplomatic post. French Guyana.

Lenore watched from atop the sweeping stairway. Like Disney's witch hearing the mirror tell her she was the fairest of them all, Lenore bent over and guffawed.

* * *

"Ten. Nine. Eight. Seven. Six. Five. Four. Three. Two. One

Happy New Year!"

At the stroke of midnight, Lenore felt no urgency to flee from Prince Wayne's embrace and kiss. Rather than turn into a tattered peasant girl, she emerged as women's committee vice-president.

# Chapter 22

"This Mess!" Elizabeth Endicott, clad in an ermine-fringed, pink satin robe, descended the main staircase. "It's past eleven o'clock." She glanced at her wafer-thin gold watch. "Why hasn't the additional cleaning staff arrived?"

"Happy New Year. New Year." Fullerton braced himself on an aluminum walker.

The peculiar tone of her husband's voice downshifted her bearing. "Happy New Year," she mumbled. "This place looks more like the aftermath of a sailor's bachelor party than a societal gala. Where's Smithers? Isn't he supposed to supervise the cleaners?"

"I dismissed Smithers."

Elizabeth squinted at Fullerton. The strangeness of his expression matched that of his speech. "You gave him today, of all days, off? Just how long do you plan on living in this mess?"

"The day off? You don't listen very well, do you? I said: I dismissed him. I've dismissed the entire staff. The manor will remain a mess until you clean it."

"Stop playing games. Where's Janine? Surely you're overdue for medication."

"My medication? The one who's going to take her medicine

is you." Fullerton handed her a manila folder. "Happy New Year. New Year."

Elizabeth opened the file. Gasping, she dropped the contents and tromped her mink-swathed foot atop them as if they were Hell's lid and her body weight alone could keep it sealed.

"I'll give you credit for one thing... Your sense of humor." The judge gleaned sadistically. "Even I laughed at the photograph of Lance Burkett in a pink tutu."

"You bastard." She grumbled through taut lips.

"Me? A bastard? Only one true bastard dwells under this roof. Do you want to tell me who she is?"

A nauseous wave enforced Elizabeth's reticence. "Tell me! Harlot!"

She cringed. In thirty cantankerous years of marriage, never had his voice oozed such rancor. "Don't want to even venture a guess?" His voice shifted to a mocking sarcasm.

Elizabeth's lips twitched.

"I'll answer the question for you then."

"Alright, I'll play your silly little game. Me. Is that what you wanted to hear?"

"Ha! Ha! Ha! Ha! Ha! Ha! Wrong. Harlot. Estelle. Your

precious little princess of a daughter. You'd be fascinated by what blood tests can prove. Harlot's too good an epithet for you. A harlot can at least commit adultery discreetly. Only a tramp—a peasant strumpet—gets knocked up in the act. Now I know why you dallied with the husband of a farmer's daughter. Now I know why you added his widow to your committee."

"I've had just about enough of this." Elizabeth picked up the folder and jabbed it into Fullerton's chest. "Love? Warmth? That's two of the things you're incapable of. I don't think I need to voice the third. Was our marriage ever but a business transaction? A cold corporate merger of the Boulez and Endicott dynasties? A bigger disaster than the one between the Pennsylvania and New York Central Railroads, I might add." Elizabeth squared her feet and placed her hands on her hips. "So I'm a harlot, huh? A tramp? A peasant strumpet? I know for a fact—a fact," Elizabeth's contorted mien acted as an exclamation point, "that Johnny Kirby and Schiller Sterling are not Main Line anomalies. Before those two even reached puberty, back when you could at least function as a man, you were Madame Misty's highest-paying customer. And I doubt very much that she charged you extra just because you could afford to pay more. So what does that make you? A whoremonger!"Elizabeth prodded. "A dog! A lover of lies."

Fullerton spat in his wife's face. "That's the second time in twelve hours, I believe. Maybe that should tell you something."

Elizabeth, out of defiance, refused to wipe away his spit.

"At least Madame Misty satisfied my natural cravings as a man." Fullerton then spoke wryly. "Natural cravings of a man." He steered his wife's gaze to a nude male statue before mustering the mobility to slap her turned cheek with the folder. "Look at these!" He poked the detective's photographs under Elizabeth's nose. "Handcuffs. Leather. Whips! Is it any damn wonder your Boulez genes spawned a pervert?"

"You miserable, old... So what do you plan on doing with those?" Scornfully, she rapped the folder with her knuckles. "Use them as grounds for divorce? At last!" Elizabeth squeezed her palms in a prayer gesture and looked upward with closed eyes. "Need I remind you," her glower resumed, "that the Boulez's command every ounce of the Endicotts' wealth and power. Furthermore," she placed thumbs in pockets and leaned forward, "divorce laws being as they are, I'll annex a major portion of that Endicott wealth. And it won't be me leaving this house either." She drew her free forefinger like a six-shooter and stabbed it in his nose. "So I suggest you shut your mouth, rehire the servants, and make sure they clean up this mess. Now!"

"Oh, don't you worry. I never dismissed the servants.

They'll be here by this afternoon. I happen to enjoy life's creature comforts as much as you, and, unlike a peasant wife," his words then spewed from his tongue like viper venom, "you're incapable of cleaning a man's house or cooking his meals!"

Elizabeth blanched.

"No. I can't deprive you of your life of luxury. But I can sack you of something you prize far more. Power! Your Junior League chairmanship, your Stanforth Heritage Society post, and especially your Cricket Club Women's Committee presidency," Fullerton then forced his sandpaper voice to resemble singing, "Nah, nah, nah, nah; nah, nah, nah, nah; hey, hey, hey, goodbye." Afterward, he grinned like a spiteful child. "As soon as we adjourn this little discussion, you will retreat to your parlor and start writing letters of resignation."

"Bravo." Elizabeth clapped. "The first sign of senility is a regression to infancy. In your case, regression to the spoilt brat that you most surely were. Resign as Windsor Women's Committee president? I don't think so. Buzz, buzz, buzz goes the bumblebee." She undulated her thumb and two fingers in Fullerton's face. "You want to act like a child? Okay. I'll treat you as one. I can sting you with far more than a costly divorce. I can have you declared senile. Mentally incompetent. One phone call. Just one phone call and I can have you committed to a home. You will be stripped of all constitutional rights. Attendants will act as your babysitter. And they won't be under your employ like Janine or Holmes. Oh no. Not by a long shot. Rather, they will wield total, humiliating power over you. So consider this conversation, confrontation, or whatever, ended." Elizabeth turned her back and stepped away.

"Ahhhh!" Fullerton roared like a laryngitis-inflicted-infected lion. Elizabeth froze.

"Really now?" He flung the folder. Sexually explicit photographs of Elizabeth and Lance fluttered about the vestibule like November leaves in a gale.

She dropped to her knees and started corralling them like a cash scramble contestant gathering currency.

"Ha! Ha! Ha! Ha! Ha! Ha!" Fullerton laughed diabolically. "Hurry now. You never know who might walk in. Those are yours, by the way. My private detective has the negatives. The fateful phone call belongs to me. One ring and they won't be on the floor— they'll grace, or shall I say, disgrace, the cover of every reputable and disreputable publication on the globe. Oh, I know what you're thinking. Your lover... No. I didn't have him killed. I'll admit that I thought about it. But his crazy son beat me to it. Seeing that it's in your best interest to play by my rules, and not even think about having me join him in the happy home. You can start writing letters of resignation."

A panting Elizabeth clutched the disheveled photographs to her breasts and confronted her tormentor. "You bastard."

"I thought we already discussed..."

"Shut up. Unlike you, I didn't live my life cloistered in aristocracy. Those committees you want to strip me of help some of the poorest, most woeful souls on Earth. Remember my trip to India? I even tried to comfort their untouchables..."

"Mary of Mercy, are you?" Fullerton clutched his collar. Thumb pointing upward, he tilted back his head. "How holy thou art."

"But you. You!" A seething Elizabeth prodded. "Hateful, bigoted bastard...are more miserable than any of them. How damned a soul must exist in that withered, wretched body. Has even the lowest dreg that you condemned from your judicial throne ever been so unhappy?"

"Touche."

Elizabeth did a double take.

"When I look back at my long life, when I look at the wealth, power, and privilege that I was supposed to enjoy, I can't imagine an unhappier, more wretched, miserable man than me. Ironic, isn't it? Here I stand looking at one of the reasons why—you, a woman who has failed so deplorably as my mate, and now, at this late hour, you will at last share with me—Hell!"

"Remember our honeymoon? My husband. Niagra Falls. Hell is forever. An eternity. Think of a lifetime as a droplet of water. Now picture Niagara Falls as trillions of metric tons of those lifetimes plunging into an abyss. That's the duration of eternal damnation." Elizabeth rubbed her cheek. "See this?" She put his spit bead before his eyes. "The extent of my sharing your cursed existence."

Fullerton slumped on his walker. Elizabeth turned and marched away.

# Chapter 23

Valentine's Day, 1970

Pat Huggins, face buried in the sports page, sat on the edge of his desk.

"I see the Seventy-Sixers won last night." Eddie Krause rapped the sales manager's newspaper.

"Yeah." Pat folded his newspaper and tucked it under his arm. "But it ain't the same since they traded Wilt Chamberlain."

"I second that. I can't even follow them anymore. Wilt Chamberlain an L.A. Laker? It just don't make sense. Sort of like saying, 'I ate a Los Angeles steak cheesesteak.'"

"I don't know about that." Pat touched his thumb to his chin and his forefinger to his cheek. "Remember, after Wilt graduated from Overbrook High here in West Philly, he went to Kansas instead of a local school. For doing that, I'll always think of Wilt as a Philly cheesesteak topped with French mustard."

Eddie lit a cigarette. "Strange way of putting it, but I understand what you're saying." Krause held the cigarette pack toward Pat. "Well, I'll tell you what's as Philadelphia as a cheesesteak smeared in Heinz ketchup..."

"Heinz is a Pittsburgh company." Pat took a cigarette from

Eddie's pack and lit it.

"At least they're Pennsylvania," Eddie countered. "Okay... It's as Philadelphia as the Mummers, the Liberty Bell, and Independence Hall. And I'll take it over the National Basketball Association any day. The Big Five at the Palestra. We got Temple, Penn, and Villanova in the top twenty, and La Salle and St. Joe's right behind. The bands. The banners. The streamers. Ten thousand screaming voices jammed into that wonderful, old building..."

"You need to add that your losing betting tickets join the streamers as confetti. Well said though, Eddie." Pat blew a smoke ring. "Talk about atmosphere. The only thing in sports to compare with a Big Five basketball showdown at the Palestra was a Brooklyn Dodgers vs. New York Giants baseball game at old Ebbets Field."

"What better way to survive a cold Philly winter than a hot Big Five doubleheader at the Palestra?"

"I agree that Big Five basketball at the Palestra makes our winters more bearable." Paul Barton approached. "But you ain't gonna enjoy our hot, sticky summers much more now that Richie Allen is gone."

"Richie Allen?" Eddie grumbled. "Good riddance."

"Good riddance?" Paul spread his arms. "The only way you bigots and boo-birds recognize a good ballplayer is if he tattoos 'good ballplayer' on his ass, then moons you with it and farts. Name a better power hitter ever to play for a Philadelphia team than Richie Allen?"

"Jimmie Foxx." Eddie flicked cigarette ashes into an ashtray. "He hit fifty-eight home runs one year. What's the most Richie Allen ever hit? Forty?"

"So forty homers is sissy stuff, huh? And Jimmie Foxx played for the A's. Unlike you, I'm not old enough to have met Ben Franklin, but I am smart enough to know about the A's."

"Jimmie Foxx played a year with the Phillies," Pat added.

"Yeah." Paul raised his right foot onto a chair. "But he damn sure never hit forty homers for the Phillies. I'll bet the Phillies never had anyone hit as many as forty homers."

"Well, you lost your bet, kid." Eddie puffed smoke upward. "Because Chuck Klein hit forty-three one year."

"At the Baker Bowl." Paul rested his right arm on his raised knee. "You probably didn't think I knew about the Baker Bowl either. Well, I also know that the Baker Bowl's right field wall was only 280 feet away. You know that, however. After all, you were there in the nineteenth century, watching them build it."

"Very funny, junior." Eddie blew smoke at Paul. "But I did see some games there. Unlike the Palestra, the Baker Bowl wasn't so venerable. One day the third base stands at that old dump collapsed and killed eleven people. Anyway, I clearly remember that high old tin wall in right field." Eddie puffed on his cigarette. "Painted in huge, big-ass letters, damn near covering the whole frickin' thing, was: 'The Phillies use Lifebuoy.' One night as a kid, me and some neighborhood buddies snuck in and painted underneath: 'But they still stink.'"

The three insurance men laughed.

"I'll tell you what." Pat crushed his cigarette. "Jimmie Foxx and Richie Allen are both damn good baseball players. But Wilt Chamberlain redefined the game of basketball."

"Exactly." Eddie dropped his butt on the floor and crushed it underfoot. "And Wilt won us a world championship. What did Richie Allen ever win for the Phillies? In his rookie year, '64, they suffered one of the worst collapses in sports history. They got worse each season thereafter, until, finally, he leaves them as ninety-nine-game losers."

"Yeah, well, the Sixers also had Hal Greer, Luke Jackson, Chet Walker, and Billy Cunningham," Paul countered. "Who have the Phillies had lately? At least Richie Allen made the games interesting."

"Assuming he'd even show up for the game at all," Eddie

countered. "I say the Phillies are better off without him. Sort of like Tony Snider. He sure could sell insurance. But aren't we better off without him?"

"I wouldn't go as far as to liken Tony Snider with Richie Allen," Pat replied. "But now that we're comparing sports stars, let me tell you something. We can talk all day about watching Big Five games instead of the Sixers. Well, back in the fifties, the Eagles were not the big football game in town. The big one was the University of Pennsylvania Quakers at Franklin Field Field. Lance Burkett meant more to the Quakers than Jimmie Foxx to the A's, Richie Allen to the Phillies, or even Wilt Chamberlain to the Sixers. I agree. Good riddance to Tony Snider. But man..." Pat looked downward, covered his eyes, and shook his head. "Do I ever miss the big guy."

Paul and Eddie looked at each other with moistening eyes.

"Yeah." The senior insurance agent stepped toward Pat's desk. "You finally hit on something even junior and I can agree on. This place sure ain't the same without him."

"And who can forget the number he did on Snider?" Paul added. "Even though he never fit in, I still don't think Snider's got this place out of his system. Didn't you get another one of his idiot postcards today?"

"Yeah. Sure did." Pat picked up a picture postcard from his

inbox and displayed a picture of Las Vegas to his workmates. "It says: 'Still thinking of you. Suckers.'"

"Suckers?" Eddie chuckled. "Lance did a bang-up job of exposing what he sucks."

"Yeah." Pat agreed. "Snider sure turned out to be a sucker in more ways than one. So now what does he take us for? After the big guy beats him out for the Vegas trip, he starts a fight with him. After losing that fight—and his job—can you believe what Snider does next? He didn't even go home to pack his toothbrush. The schmuck went straight to the airport and hopped on the first Vegas-bound flight. Now he's a Keno caller at some back desert motel. Paul, your wife just had a baby. Is that what you want your son to grow up to be? A Keno caller?"

"Oh, please." Paul covered his ears and shook his head.

"Ah, get a load of this!" Eddie Krause angrily shook Pat's newspaper. "What's this world coming to? Remember right before Lance got killed? Walter Caan, that scum-bag rapist that some sleazebag lawyer sprang on a technicality."

"Who can forget?" Pat pulled his face and shook his head. "He's let out of prison, heads straight for the state line, and eight hours later gets arrested for raping a thirteen-year-old."

"Well, listen to this." Krause then read aloud a newspaper

editorial. "Despite the enlightened compassion of the previous decade, bitter reactionaries still dwell among us. Case in point are the vengeance-crazed vigilantes who screamed for the blood of Walter Caan like the maddened mob before Pontius Pilate. What the unenlightened fail to grasp is that crime is an artificial growth grafted onto human life by the development of societies and governments. Our government institutionalized unjust inequality of wealth from the very moment of its foundation. Even after the Revolution, Americans legally bartered and sold African slaves like cattle. The Civil War, rather than freeing black people from the bondage of slavery, merely reconsigned them into the oppression of systemic racism. Neither are disadvantaged Whites immune to the cudgel of corporate fuhrers. Walter Caan is but a scion of a system that substitutes selling overpriced and defective goods for mask and gun robbery. How can we possibly end crime in the streets without first attacking crime in the suites? Imagine the disillusion of Walter Caan's grandfather. After escaping a life of impoverishment imposed by some monocled baron, he first sights the Statue of Liberty through a crack in a ship's steerage. Then some cigar-chomping plutocrat condemns him to fourteen-hour days working in a lung-defiling mill just to pay rent on a rat-infested tenement using a tin pail as plumbing. That environment spawned Walter Caan. Can any enlightened, socially conscious mind possibly deem Walter Caan's acts as criminal? No. The true criminals are the ones who created his oppressive environment, and the American capitalist government is a co-conspirator. Walter Caan's raping of a banker's thirteen-year-old daughter, therefore, represents no less an act of legitimate rebellion than the patriots who tossed British tea into the Boston harbor. True justice would be jailing all of us as accomplices of systematic exploitation, while the Walter Caans of the world run free to reassert their stolen selfhood."

"Ugh, ugh." Paul Barton bent over and pantomimed puking by putting forefinger in throat.

"What kind of shit is this?" Pat snatched the newspaper and wryly twisted his face as he glanced at the words. "So concerned, law-abiding citizens, wanting a safe, decent society to raise their families in, are unenlightened, vengeance-crazed vigilantes?"

Paul leaned over and perused the newspaper. "And imagine making a reference to Christ with that thing." He tapped Walter Caan's mug-shot. "Good grief, Charlie Brown. Hey, if anyone could've killed Lance Burkett, it's him and not his skinny thirteen-year-old son."

"Walter Caan probably did kill people we don't know about, but he's got the best alibi on Earth for not killing Lance Burkett," Pat lit another cigarette. "He was in jail at the time."

"Too bad Judge Fullerton Endicott didn't sentence him,"

Paul added. "Then I bet that poor thirteen-year-old girl wouldn't've been raped."

"Actually," Eddie sat in a chair and placed ankle on knee. "Judge Endicott did sentence him. Sent him away for life, no parole. Blame the sleaze lawyer that sprung him on a loophole."

"I wish they'd throw that lawyer in the same jail cell with Caan." Paul placed hands on hips.

"No. I'll tell you what would be better." Pat stood and prodded. "Lock the lawyer in a jail cell with the parents of the thirteen-year-old girl. That damn lawyer already knows what Walter Caan is all about. Mr. Sleaze just wanted to win his case and enhance his reputation. Rather lock up the idiot who wrote this editorial with Caan."

"Yeah." Krause snickered. "Then at least his asshole will get opened up a bit so that he can shit in a toilet instead of on the pages of our newspapers. Frank Rizzo said it best: 'A liberal is a conservative who hasn't been mugged yet.'"

"I agree," Pat replied. "I also agree with something Paul mentioned. I don't think Lance's skinny kid did him in either."

"Why do you say that?" Krause asked.

"I didn't know the kid that well. He was always quiet, a bit different, but a good kid nonetheless."

"Sure. Many people have preconceived ideas of what, say, bank presidents look like, or teamsters, or priests, and Caan's mug surely says, psychopathic criminal. But don't evil people have a knack for deception?" Eddie raised his palms. "How often when some mass murderer is finally captured, everyone who knew him says," Eddie wryly garbled his voice, "he was such an ordinary guy. I never suspected a thing." Eddie resumed normal speech and spread his arms. "Damn. Give me a break, Pat. Lance's loony kid did him in."

"I admitted that he was different," Pat held up his palms, "but he was different because he was a deeper thinker than most thirteen-year-olds."

"All the more reason that he plotted the damn thing," Eddie retorted.

"The overwhelming evidence says that if Geoff Burkett did kill his father, he acted on the spur of the moment. Intelligent people seldom act rashly. Look," Pat opened his hands. "I realize that Lance never established much of a rapport with the kid. You know that sports meant the world to the big guy, and his son was a klutz from the word go. Lance identified more with his second son, Myles, who, if not bound to follow in his father's footsteps, at least shared his interests. That I don't think Geoffrey was mentally or morally capable of murdering his father may not mean much to you. But consider this." Pat pointed at them. "Did he have the physical ability? Think about it, stalking then wielding a fatal blow to an All-American athlete outweighing him by more than a hundred pounds? I think not."

"Walter Caan sure could. Look at the size of this guy." Paul pointed to the newspaper picture.

"Walter Caan was in jail at the time." Pat put his hands in his pockets.

"Alright Sherlock," Eddie grumbled. "If you're such a brilliant detective, why don't you tell us who you think murdered Lance Burkett?"

"His wife. Without a doubt, his wife."

"His wife?" Eddie waved off Pat. "I thought you said the murder required athletic ability."

"Ahhh..." Pat wiggled his forefinger. "Lenore Burkett has a mind that can overcome any obstacle."

"I sure can't remember the big guy ever saying anything nice about her," Paul added. "You didn't see them together as much as I did. That relationship was cold." Pat covered his chest and pantomimed shivering. "Arctic cold."

"Then why didn't they just divorce?" Paul asked. "After all, isn't that what you and Henny did?"

"Money," Pat answered.

"I'm starting to see what you mean." Eddie allowed his cigarette to dangle from his lower lip. "If she divorced him, Lance couldn't have given her dick. But by killing him..."

"All that insurance money." Paul's eyes twinkled.

"Another thing, the big guy didn't give a shit about Main Line society." Pat lit a cigarette. "Man, his wife, she was obsessed with it. All the time she was married to him, the only status she ever climbed to was pariah. Lenore always had someone to blame for her shortcomings, and don't think she didn't blame Lance for her social setbacks. Don't you find it suspicious, that, no sooner is the big guy gone, than she rises to president of the Windsor Cricket Club Woman's Committee? That's Main Line society's most eminent post. A title restricted to a Dorothy Madison or an Elizabeth Endicott. But Lenore Burkett? Normally a woman of her status gets committed just for dreaming about it. Yet, she got it."

"Whatever did happen to Elizabeth Endicott?" Eddie asked. "All of those powerful social commands..."

"Maybe she made a New Year's resolution," Paul answered. "After all, that's the day she abdicated them all."

"I guess only Elizabeth Endicott will ever know because she

sure isn't saying why." Eddie flicked cigarette ashes. "How about Wayne Madison? The Main Line's most eligible widower. What does a classy, cultured gentleman like him see in Lenore Burkett? We can only open up a porno centerfold and jerk off, Wayne Madison can open it up and say, 'I want her', and he gets her. After all, that's what Argus Garvos does, and Wayne's a decade younger and just as rich."

"Lenore Burkett conniving her way to Wayne Madison doesn't surprise me in the least," Pat said. "Mr. Madison may be the Bachelor of the seventies, but, back in the fifties, the most sought-after bachelor was University of Pennsylvania's dashing all-American quarterback Lance Burkett. Back then, he could make a woman, any woman, swoon, just by looking at her."

"Don't I remember!" Eddie looked at Paul. "Too bad you never saw Lance's number one gal. Melanie Beach. Va-va-va-Voom!" Lust shined from the old man's face.

"Oh, but I did see her," Paul nodded. "At Lance's funeral. I don't know how she looked back in the fifties, but when I spotted her at the sight gravesite— I was holding hands with my wife at the time, I'm ashamed to say— my eyes couldn't help but ever so gently remove her black dress. Now don't get me wrong guys, Lenore was a good-looking gal — but Melanie Beach? Man! If Lenore's scheming beat her out for Lance, then, yes, she's capable of anything. Wayne Madison. The Cricket Club Presidency. Even killing her husband."

"I gotta hand it to you, Pat." Eddie raised his arms in mock surrender. "You present a compelling case against Lenore. Nevertheless, you still haven't exonerated Geoffrey."

"I was Lance's best friend. He told me things he didn't tell anyone else. Yes, Lance didn't have much of a relationship with Geoffrey, but, good guy that he was, he only told me this: Lenore deliberately got pregnant with Geoffrey to force him to marry her."

"Couldn't he have just sent her off for an abortion?"

"You're a product of the late sixties and now early seventies, Paul," Pat answered. "Back in the fifties, you knocked a gal up—you married her. Simpler solutions for a simpler time."

"Are you trying to tell me that Lenore killed her husband, and then framed her son?" Eddie crossed his arms and tilted his head.

"That's exactly what I'm saying."

"Oh, bullshit." Eddie waved him off. "No one—"

Pat held up his arm in the halt gesture. "Admittedly, I don't know Lenore real well, but I sure knew Lance. I could just see it in his eyes that he was married to no ordinary woman."

"But her own son?" Paul asked.

"Absolutely. Lenore is a user. Once a mark fulfills her purpose, she casts 'em off. No deposit. No return. Geoff got her Lance. Mission accomplished. Get out of my sight. You're a thorn in my side."

"What about her other son? Myles?" Eddie flicked aside his cigarette butt.

"Read the sports page of the Suburban and Stanforth Times. He's no Lance Burkett, but, hey, you'll usually find something there about Myles. That gives Lenore a step up on the other Main Line mothers. Yet as soon as Myles stops starring in sports— look out! She'll start treating him as excess baggage as well... Well..." Pat checked his watch. "It's about that time."

"Since when did you," Eddie pointed, "ever need a watch to tell you that it was that time?"

Pat, ignoring the barb, reached into his desk drawer and pulled out a bottle of Evan Williams Bourbon and three shot glasses. He poured and handed two to his salesmen. The sales manager held his full glass aloft. "To the last of the real men. Lance Burkett."

"To Lance Burkett. A real man." They touched glasses and quaffed.

# Chapter 24

A nondescript office belied District Attorney Derrick Anvil's powerful post. His desk was conventional business furniture, metal with an imitation oak veneer top, functional drawers, and a typewriter stand. Atop that desk, he displayed the obligatory pictures of his wife, two sons, and a daughter. On his wall hung a picture of then Police Commissioner Frank Rizzo awarding him detective of the year, Fullerton Endicott congratulating him for earning his University of Pennsylvania School of Law degree, and a photo of himself posing with Frank Rizzo as Mayor of Philadelphia and champion boxer Joe Frazier. Several plaques honoring his police and legal achievements joined those photos. A two-foot-high trophy for coaching a champion Boy's Club boxing team sat atop a metal filing cabinet.

The remaining hair atop the District Attorney's pate arrowed toward his intense close-set eyes, double-ridged nose, small mouth, and pointed chin. "You said you had something to say of utmost importance." He gestured at two chairs. "Nothing is so important that it can't be said in five minutes."

Dr. Tryvye and Scotch Sutton sat. "The reason for this meeting is," the psychiatrist folded his hands on the district attorney's desk, "to inform you that the psychiatric board of Harlond

State Mental Hospital and myself have deemed Geoffrey Burkett sane. We will, therefore, be releasing him on an outpatient basis into the custody of Mr. Sutton."

Only a deep breath revealed any reaction from Derrick Anvil.

The District Attorney's reticence made Dr. Tryvye nervous. He spoke faster. "Moreover, we determined that Geoffrey Burkett did not murder his father. So you must now reopen the Lance Burkett case."

"Ah ha," the district attorney nodded.

"Yes, um," Dr. Tryvye twitched, then flapped his hands. "First, we administered a polygraph exam." The psychiatrist looked deeply into the D.A.'s eyes. "Now, I know that polygraph results are inadmissible in a court of law. Although, as you're no doubt aware, the law enforcement community does respect them. Nevertheless," Dr. Tryvye rambled on, "the courts reject them because the suspect's conscious mind is capable of denying the reality known only within the subconscious mind to the extent of believing his lies to the point of fooling the polygraph machine."

Without changing his expression, Derrick Anvil placed his clenched hands atop his desk.

Dr. Tryvye nibbled his fingernails before continuing.

"Therefore, I administered the ultimate test of truth. I reached into the boy's subconscious mind via hypnosis. You see, via hypnosis, I achieved the manifest analytical realization that Geoffrey Burkett was telling the truth. He knew nothing of the literal dynamics of his father's murder." The psychiatrist strummed his fingers on the desktop.

After thirty unnerving seconds of silence, the district attorney spoke. "Your five minutes are up. In all due respect to your profession, Dr. Tryvye, and from what I have read, you're world-renowned. I have dedicated my last thirty years to either enforcing the law, solving crimes, or trying criminals. Hypnosis? Schmokus hocus pocus. I deal only with empirical evidence. Hard facts. If the facts didn't overwhelmingly say Geoff Burkett murdered his father, do you think I would've closed the case? In Lance Burkett, we're not talking about some back alley, ghetto dope pusher. He was a former Ivy League All-American quarterback. A public figure. The police force does now employ psychiatrists and psychologists to probe the criminal mind and thus give us intangible leads. But who does the actual investigating? Detectives. Not psychiatrists. So, please, Dr. Tryvye. You stick to your job and I'll stick to mine." District Attorney Anvil gestured at the door.

"Ahhh," Dr. Tryvye pointed to the ceiling. "I do have objective evidence. At first, Geoffrey's testimony under hypnosis..."

Derrick Anvil stood and leaned forward with his arms braced on the desk.

The psychiatrist spoke faster, "...cast some doubts on his innocence. He left a gap between the confrontation witnessed by his younger brother and Donald Frankincense, and his arrest in the linen closet. I reexamined his medical file." Dr. Tryvye flipped open a folder and slid it toward the D.A. "The boy suffered a severe concussion. Enough to render him unconscious. I interviewed the Frankincense boy under the auspices of his father. Here," the psychiatrist took a page from the folder, put his forefinger on the bottom, and held it before the D.A., "Dr. Frankincense's signature. That confirms his son's testimony that Geoffrey Burkett fell unconscious while his father, Lance Burkett, banged his head against the wall."

"Care to tell me what a concussion is?" Derrick Anvil crossed his arms.

"A concussion is a physical manifestation of the brain rebounding against the inner skull."

"Exactly. Look. I know because I was a boxer and now a boxing coach. What you describe is exactly what occurs when a boxer gets knocked out. Do you know how often I've seen a fighter get knocked cold, only to get back up and beat the ten-second count?"

Dr. Tryvye and Scotch said nothing.

"More times than I care to remember. So, yes, the Frankincense kid did see Geoffrey go down. He just didn't see him get back up. If anything, you just buried your boy deeper. The brain rattle probably triggered his crazed act. So don't plan on releasing Geoffrey Burkett anytime soon. Please excuse me." The D.A. sat. "I have a lot of paperwork to catch up on." He looked down and jotted on a form.

"Um, excuse me, sir, um," Dr. Tryvye continued. "What you don't understand is, um, the decisions of Harland state are out of your jurisdiction. We're not here for your permission, but only to inform you of Geoffrey Burkett's imminent release, so that you can reopen the case and find the true perpetrator."

"Out of my jurisdiction?" Derrick Anvil sprung to his feet and dropped his prize fountain pen. He ignored it rolling off his desk and plunking on the floor. "OK." His eyes bore into the psychiatrist.

Dr. Tryvye blanched.

"You want to put an ax murderer back on my streets? Go right ahead." The D.A. flipped his hands. "Let him out of your happy home ...Do that and I'll put him away in my not-so-happy home in the time it takes Joe Frazier to throw a left hook." He shifted his glower. "You're a lawyer, Mr. Sutton. I know what you're thinking. Double jeopardy. Well, forget it. Your grandson was never acquitted of murder. We never even charged him. And, seeing that murder has no statute of limitations, I can arrest the little shit anytime I want." The D.A. prodded at Scotch. "The only reason we didn't press charges was because we figured committing him to a funny farm would put him away longer than some bleeding heart liberal judge would jail him. But if you care a shred for your grandson, you won't even think of trying the criminal justice route. Because until some liberal springs him, and that could take years, I have the power to make his life very, very uncomfortable." The D.A. pursed his lips and narrowed his eyes.

For five pregnant seconds, the grandfather and the psychiatrist wanly looked at each other.

Dr. Tryvye then shrugged; Scotch nodded resignation. They both took a final glance at the marble-faced District Attorney before slumping toward the door.

"I don't think so." Hand in hand with Geoffrey Burkett, Elizabeth Endicott entered the office.

Scotch tingled as a skeptical child would on seeing Santa Claus emerge from his fireplace.

Dr. Tryvye removed his half-eye spectacles, rubbed his eyes, and then returned them to his Byzantine nose. Derrick Anvil straitened straightened his collar while snapping to military attention.

"Hi, granddad. Hi Dr. Tryvye. This is Aunt Lizzie. That real nice lady I told you about."

"She's," Scotch's finger groped, "your Aunt Lizzie?"

"Ya. You know, the one who always visits me and brings me all those neat rockets and all."

Elizabeth nodded to Scotch, then turned and noticed a lip quivering D.A. "Ever vigilant to the end. I like that. My husband, of course, would expect no less."

The D.A. relaxed.

"Nevertheless, you can direct your resolve to another matter. This case is closed." Elizabeth opened her alligator leather briefcase and handed the D.A. a form. "An official pardon from Governor Stanton. Geoffrey Burkett is absolved of all charges. He may go home with Mr. Sutton."

"Yippee!" Geoffrey ran and hugged his grandfather.

Derrick Anvil looked into the society matron's eyes and felt like a scolded ten-year-old child.

He glanced at the Fullerton Endicott photograph. A four-decade-old memory of schoolyard bullies intimidating him caused that picture to rise eighteen inches up on the wall. Then he recalled his first boxing lesson ... "Geoffrey." The D.A. pointed at the boy. "Please step outside."

"No." Geoffrey squeezed Scotch. "Aunt Lizzie said I could go home with Granddad."

"Officer Carr!" The D.A. shouted to a uniformed policeman. "Please look after this kid."

"No. But I want to stay with you."

"Better go with him," Scotch whispered.

Geoff reluctantly left the office with the crewcut rookie patrolman.

"That's the last bit of sympathy I show him." Derrick Anvil pointed at the now-closed office door. "In all deference to you, Mrs. Endicott, your husband put me through law school and helped me secure this title because he had confidence in both my willingness and my ability to uphold law and order. My sworn duty is to protect the public. I'm afraid I'm going to have to override both you and the governor and not subject the citizenry to an ax murderer."

"But the governor Pardoned ... "

Elizabeth silenced Scotch by holding up the halt sign.

"Mr. Sutton," the D.A. continued. "Need I remind you that Geoffrey Burkett is no longer a legal member of your family? Your daughter signed him over as a ward of the state. That makes him mine. Until he is officially adopted, he will remain in the state's custody. I have the power to put him anywhere I like. I can make him the most notorious criminal's cellmate. Even Walter Caan."

Elizabeth winced.

"So please," the D.A. prodded. "Cut the nonsense, and, for everyone's sake, leave Geoffrey Burkett in the funny farm." Scotch's forlorn expression bolstered the D.A. "And just where do you get off anyway, Mr. Sutton?"

"Huh?"

"Just where do you get off, thinking you can take care of the little creep better than an army of shrinks can?" The D.A. prodded at Scotch. "Don't think that I'm unaware of your son Charles. He is, for all intents and purposes, a three-time felon. You twice plea-bargained for university expulsion in lieu of felony drug or arson charges. Last New Year's Eve he got busted selling drugs to an undercover narcotics agent. Another felony. Another deal. This time he agreed to serve in the Army. So what if the governor pardoned the boy? I can still open the case to find the true perp. Guess who becomes our number one suspect?"

Scotch shrugged.

"Your daughter. All the motive in the world, plus a suspect alibi. Who gained more from Lance Burkett's death than her? Windsor Cricket Club Woman's Committee president? Come on, Mr. Sutton. As a lawyer myself, I admire your achievements in the field. Some would even credit you as a pillar of the community. But the Suttons just aren't in a league with the Madisons or Endicotts." Derrick Anvil glanced at Elizabeth. "Or the Boulez's." He put his right foot forward and pointed both his forehead and finger at Scotch. "And you know that. So maybe you can tell me, just how she managed stepping so high out of her league. I'd love to know." The D.A. crossed his arms with thumbs pointing upward.

Scotch clenched his fists, breathed deeply, then tucked his thumbs under his belt.

"Mrs. Endicott." The D.A. shifted to the society matron. "Despite my curiosity, I respect you enough not to ask you how or why Lenore Burkett managed to assume your post. It's irrelevant anyway. Her son and not herself committed the murder. That we're convinced of. I do once again wish to thank you for your family's support, both in finance and influence. Nevertheless, I'm sure you respect that I have a job to do. Dr. Tryvye," the D.A. pointed at the psychiatrist. "You're entitled to make the boy just as comfortable as you like in your big happy home. Just make sure he stays there. So if you would all excuse me," the D.A. buried his head in a police report.

Scotch stepped toward the D.A.'s desk. "I resent any implications that a member of my family could've murdered my son-in-law. Nevertheless, in many ways, you do speak the truth. It hurts to admit that I wasn't a perfect parent. I exercised the best intentions, just not the best judgment. The depression changed the perspective of many of us. We wanted our children to have the best of what we didn't have at all. To do this, I threw myself into my law practice. When not dedicating my time to the firm, it was the farm. Chicken farming meant more than carrying on a family tradition, I felt that a farm represented the best environment to raise a child. Unfortunately, my daughter always wanted more and my son rebelled. It took my new foreman, Mr. Norman Bell, to show me the things that matter most. I know that you don't much believe in second chances, Mr. Anvil. But I do. I now know what matters most. I'm going to stay retired from law. Additionally, I'm promoting Norman Bell to farm director. He will run the entire operation. I wish to dedicate my remaining years to what matters most. My family. Dolly. And my grandson."

"Touching." Mr. Anvil looked up from his desk. "So touching that I'm going to grant you your wish. You may dedicate the rest of your life to your wife and grandson. Myles. The ax murderer, however, will remain in custody. I'll give you a choice. Harlond State Mental Hospital or Carlyle State Prison."

Scotch gave the hardened D.A. a final plaintive glance, turned to an equally despondent Dr. Tryvye, and then trudged toward the door.

"Obdurate 'till the end." Elizabeth Endicott strode to the desk. "Mr. Anvil, you truly are a man of my husband's calling. Which is why I anticipated your move. Is this satisfactory?" Elizabeth placed an official form before the D.A.

Derrick Anvil's eyes bulged and lips quavered as he read the governor's signature, confirming the adoption of Geoffrey Burkett by Scotch Sutton. Geoffrey no longer belongs to the state.

"Get back here, you rascal!" Patrolman Carr yelled.

"Granddad! Granddad!" Geoffrey ran into the office. "Why do I have to stay here?" He hugged his grandfather. "Aunt Lizzie said I can go home with you."

"Don't worry. Aunt Lizzie is right." Scotch looked at the moist-eyed society matron and winked. "You can go home with me. Right now." Walking out of the office with his exonerated grandson, Scotch next turned to a beaming psychiatrist. "I know that you've never much believed in Jesus. But what do you say now?"

"Ah hum." Dr. Tryvye cleared his throat. "Scrupulous

analysis of certain unaccountable phenomena sometimes indicates a potential metaphysical intervention." He smiled and looked upward.

"I sure hope you believe in Jesus." The D.A. stood and wagged his finger at Scotch. "Because you're gonna need him. You're taking an ax murderer into your home."

GOTTERDAMMERUNG

A miniature University of Pennsylvania gonfalon waved from Wayne's Ferrari antenna as he drove along Stanforth's twisting residential lanes. His lady rode beside him. Her son's head intruding from the backseat broke their romantic spell. Soon enough they approached the forty-seven-acre, Madison estate main entrance, an imposing pink marble and Istrian stone archway imported from the Palazzo Bevilacqu-Lamassa at Verona. Limestone seahorses and a sculpture of Neptune armed with a three-prong spear topped the arch. A uniformed guard nodded to Wayne, then opened the arabesque wrought iron gates. The Ferrari entered. Sculpted stone courses with shell-shaped fountain basins designed by Giacomo Vignola for the Villa Lante near Viterbo flanked the entrance drive. The Ferrari soon circled a reflecting pool centered by a sword-drawn knight riding a swan. That Wayne Madison designed for Marion Endicott to sculpt.

The grounds served as a mere appetizer for Lenore's true

visual feast. His dwelling.

Wayne's triple-storey Queen Anne-style mansion featured prominent Dutch gables. Leathery ivy embellished the exterior's synthesis of red brick and stone. White-painted wooden window frames perfected the picture. The Ferrari stopped under the home's entrance pergola. "Well, Myles, what do you say about all of this?" Lenore asked.

"Ya. I guess it's better than that big dump in Cape May."

Wayne sighed and tapped his forehead before lighting the vehicle, circling it, and opening Lenore's door. Lending a chivalrous hand, he helped her disembark. Suddenly Myles slithered over the front seat and burst between them, breaking Wayne and Lenore's handhold.

A black and white-clad English butler opened the front door formally as a palace guard from Alice in Wonderland. Myles stormed past him.

"Myles!" Lenore shouted.

"Oh, don't you worry about him," Wayne said. "Let him go. He'll find plenty of places to have fun playing hide and seek."

"What if he breaks something?"

"I'm sure my staff can look after my valuables. Come."

Wayne gestured toward the front door.

Lenore complied.

Suddenly Wayne doffed his jacket, threw it on the threshold, and swept his arms in a grand entrance invitation.

Lenore chuckled. "Oh, Wayne." She started bending for his jacket.

"No. I insist." Placing his hand on her back, he gently guided her over the jacket and into his home.

"Well. What do you think? Like it more than my dump in Cape May?"

"Yes, of course." Lenore rotated her head, absorbing his vestibule's arrangement of colonial American and British antique furniture, and its display of cultivated sculpture and painting. Abundant freshly cut flowers delighted her eyes and nose. "No, I mean. Um. Your house in Cape May is wonderful." She scratched her right temple. "I'm sorry, please forgive Myles. But Wayne," she reasserted her posture, "everything here is so... Overwhelming. That's the word I'm looking for. Overwhelming."

"Thank you, Lenore." Wayne took her hand. "And please quit aching your pretty head over Myles." Wayne relieved her distress with a gentle chuckle. "Okay. I admit." He turned and braced her shoulders. "Sometimes I find him vexing. Yet I'm sure one fine day soon," Wayne's eyes warmly linked with hers, "he'll come around." They embraced.

Feeling like a child touring toy land, Lenore's buoyant steps followed her beau through his museum-like home. Dutch wall murals. Ceilings painted like an Italian Renaissance church. A music room featuring a 17th-century German harpsichord and a harp hailing from Louis XVI France. A library with built-in mahogany shelves boasting leather-bound, first editions of English classics. After ascending a cantilevered spiral staircase of Spanish Baroque design, Lenore found herself in Wayne's bedroom. "I must say." She scanned the four walls. "You sure are a man of international tastes. That Chinese vase." She turned her gaze to the room's northeast cover corner.

"It must be ancient."

"From the Ming dynasty." Wayne raised his chin. "And that Japanese Samurai sword," he pointed to the west wall, "is just as old." Taking her hand, he sat her next to him on his bed: formerly Scarlett O'Hara and Rhett Butler's from the set of Gone With the Wind. "Although possessions don't define the man, I won't say that I've never enjoyed them." Wayne looked toward Lenore, but not at her. "What I'm trying to say is, that I used to enjoy them. But without Dorothy to share them with, this chamber, my entire home for that matter, might as well be empty. Barren. Effete."

Lenore blanched.

"Ironic isn't it?" Wayne continued. "Dorothy and I were the Cricket Club's king and queen. Well, here I am, still Windsor's president. Yet now I sit next to its new queen." He pointed at Lenore, "you, the new Women's Committee president. Today, Valentine's Day, of all days. So I can't think of a better day to ask you to join me on my throne. Share with me this kingdom."

"Wayne." Lenore gasped. "Are you?" She felt her heart tingle and rise. "Yes, Lenore. I am. Will you marry me?"

"Oh, Wayne." Amorously she embraced him. Behind his back, her right fist pumped like a baseball pitcher's after striking out the final World Series batter. "Yes." Her lips caressed his ear as she spoke. "Yes, of course I'll marry you."

Their passionate hug ripened into a frenzied kiss. Under the bed's lace canopy, they rolled. Wayne rubbed his chest over her nipples and laughed.

"Wonderful!" He climbed to his knees and pinned her to the beige satin, gold velvet floral crested bedspread. "Wonderful." About to kiss her again, he noticed that her expression said anything but 'wonderful'.

"What's wrong?" He swung his feet to the silk Tabriz rug and sat on the edge of the bed.

Lenore, elbow on knee, chin in palm, sat beside him, ignoring the bed's satin valance draping her shoulder.

"Myles. He's been through so much already. This could prove traumatic. I don't know, Wayne. Maybe we should wait until he gets used to us." Lenore sighed and dropped her head into her hands.

"Nonsense." Wayne's left hand clasped hers. "What Myles needs is a man's influence." He raised her chin with his right forefinger.

"But he's not yet ready to accept you."

"Agreed. However. I've got the perfect solution." Lenore suddenly flushed and beamed.

"Let's enroll him in Bunker Hill Military Academy. There he'll not only get the manly direction he needs, but they'll keep him too busy to fret over us. By spring break he'll be all too happy to see us together."

"I don't know Wayne. Bunker Hill Military Academy. Isn't it a bit...?"

"Oh come on Lenore, it's not as harsh as it sounds. After all, Bunker Hill is close enough for him to walk home on Sundays. It offers lots of sports. And I'll bet he'll love the marching and military drills. You always complain that his grades could be higher. Well,

Bunker Hill is noted for instilling a sense of duty and discipline in a boy. The Endicott's oldest son, Mitchell, graduated from Bunker Hill, and now he's about to run for governor. Pundits say that a successful term will make him a candidate for the Republican Presidential nomination. Myles is in what? Seventh grade?"

"Sixth," Lenore answered.

"O.K. Sixth. Well after six- and- a half years of Bunker Hill, I'll have no trouble getting him into Penn."

"I can't see Penn ever turning away a Burkett," Lenore replied.

"Won't Bunker Hill have him well prepared?"

"Oh, Wayne, yes, of course. And do you know what else?" Wayne shrugged.

"I love you." They kissed.

Three tongue-fluttering minutes later, Wayne stood, extended his hands, and helped Lenore to her feet.

"I take it we have a done deal then?"

"Yes. Yes, of course." Lenore wrapped her arms around his neck. "Let me go find Myles. Now I can't wait to tell him the news. You wait here. I'll go find him."

Lenore, with the help of the butler, cook, chauffeur, and two chambermaids vainly searched the mansion's fifty-two rooms for her wayward son. A frustrated Lenore finally trudged back to Wayne's bedroom. She spotted a trickle of viscous crimson leaking under the door. Nervously, she creaked it open.

"Oh God." Her sickened voice croaked from her chest. "No. No. No." She covered her face and fell to her knees. Vomit and bile burst through her fingers. Briefly, she inspected the black disgorge on her palms, then glanced at the slaughter. Fainting, her nose struck the blood-flooded floor.

The shock granted her fifteen seconds of mercy. She crawled to the bed, grasped a post, and pulled herself to her feet. Her mind began to codify that the dead, disemboweled body belonged to Wayne. His small intestine choked what remained of his throat. Lenore could count all seven of his cervical vertebrae. The killer had slashed off Wayne's member and clamped it between his bared teeth. She keeled over and retched blood. Head oscillating wildly, she somehow noticed that Wayne's Samurai sword was missing from its wall mount.

"Mommy."

"Myles? Myles, is that you?"

"Mommy." The brat pushed open the closet door like Dracula would his coffin. Myles emerged. He toted Wayne's blood-soaked Samurai sword.

"He was no good for you, Mommy. I couldn't let him wreck us no more. You'd never tear us apart by sending me to Bunker Hill. It was his idea." Myles pointed at Wayne's butchered corpse. "Only his."

"How did, how did you," Lenore's irregular heart palpitations blocked her speech.

"I hid under the bed. I heard everything he said." Myles approached his gasping mother. "I had to save us from him."

"Your father," Lenore pointed at him. "Was it? Did you?"

"Daddy was no good for us. He treated you bad, and he didn't care nothing about me no more."

"So it was you, and not..." Lenore jittered her finger like a dying victim pointing to her murderer.

"Geoffrey was no good for us too. You always said so. I knew we'd be happier without him. So I made them think he did it."

"But this house. Everything. It could've been ours. Someday it would've all been yours."

"I don't care, Mommy." Myles strode to Lenore. "I don't need a bunch 'a stuff." He handed her the Samurai sword. "I only want you." He hugged her. "I only want just you and me to be happy together."

A mental flash spread the loss, the scandal, and the upcoming legal hassles before her like a line of dirty laundry. The next vision showed Elizabeth Endicott pitching her out the Cricket Club's back door and into a pond of chicken shit. Fowl prancing over her fetid body pecked out her eyes. Above the clucking, Lenore heard Betty Kirby and Hillary Sterling's derisive laughter. The last laugh.

"I did it all because I love you, Mommy."

"You..." With two hands overhead, Lenore raised the sword. "Bastard!" She thrust it into her son's back. The blade ripped open his ribs.

Myles collapsed on her feet, too dazed to feel pain.

"I love you, Mommy." The blood spouted like a geyser, soon mingling with Wayne's. Myles collapsed. Wayne and Myles faced each other in cataleptic slumber.

"Myles?" Lenore bent over, wrapped her right arm around his inert chest, and braced her left hand behind his flaccid neck. "Myles?" She lifted his breathless head to her breasts. Her son's pupils and irises were hidden under his eye socket's north-west corners. His corneas were blank as a photographic negative.

"Myles? Myles? Myles!" She cradled and rocked her son.

"My baby! My baby! My baby! Answer me! Answer me! Answer me!" His jaw hung agape, his tongue a limp flap.

"No!" She dropped him. He splashed into a blood puddle.

"No-o-o-o!" Fingers clawing her hair, palms scratching her eyes, she screamed.

Gradually, she uncovered her eyes and looked down.

"No!" Her son lay in his blood, still as a goldfish floating atop its tank. Lenore drew the sword from his back fervently as Sigmund pulling the sword Notung from the tree trunk.

"Ahh!" She screamed and thrust the sword into her gut. Although aware of her inability to breathe, she felt no desire for air. Through the haze, Lenore saw her blood mix with her son's and fiancé's. She smiled. She next felt her head shatter like a light bulb

Darkness. Only darkness.

***

Lenore stood before the fire. It burned from molten rocks rather than logs. The smoke billows shrouded its light. The bursts of heat were too constant to move her. She belonged here and here she would stay.

She knew who was its king. She had no hope of being its queen.

# **About The Author**

Gregory T. Glading wrote the first word of Severed Ties shortly after finishing his first novel, '64 Intruder. The final edit and transcription were approved after completing Chords of Time, Darka's Quest, and Rivka's Revelation. Gregory T. Glading is currently writing his sixth novel. A Temple University graduate, the author has visited over forty countries. He is a retired hall-of-fame professional wrestler and was awarded the Order Of The Spur for skill, cunning, dash, and fervor in combat with the 1st Battalion, 12th Cavalry Regiment, 1st Cavalry Division in Iraq.